Invisible Links

Invisible Links

Selma Lagerlöf

Translated by
Pauline Bancroft Flach

Ægypan Press

Selma Lagerlöf lived from 1858 to 1940.

Invisible Links
A publication of
ÆGYPAN PRESS
www.aegypan.com

Table of Contents

The Spirit of Fasting and Petter Nord

I

I can see before me the little town, friendly as a home. It is so small that I know its every hole and corner, am friends with all the children and know the name of everyone of its dogs. Who ever walked up the street knew to which window he must raise his eyes to see a lovely face behind the panes, and who ever strolled through the town park knew well whither he should turn his steps to meet the one he wished to meet.

One was as proud of the beautiful roses in the garden of a neighbor, as if they had grown in one's own. If anything mean or vulgar was done, it was as great a shame as if it had happened in one's own family; but at the smallest adventure, at a fire or a fight in the marketplace, one swelled with pride and said: "Only see what a community! Do such things ever happen anywhere else? What a wonderful town!"

In my beloved town nothing ever changes. If I ever come there again, I shall find the same houses and shops that I knew of old; the same holes in the pavements will cause my downfall; the same stiff hedges of lindens, the same clipped lilac bushes will captivate my fascinated gaze. Again shall I see the old Mayor who rules the whole town walking down the street with elephantine tread. What a feeling of security there is in knowing that you are walking there! And deaf old Halfvorson will still be digging in his garden, while his eyes, clear as water, stare and wander as if they would say: "We have investigated everything, everything; now, earth, we will bore down to your very center."

But one who will not still be there is little, round Petter Nord: the little fellow from Värmland, you know, who was in Halfvorson's shop; he who amused the customers with his small mechanical inventions and his white mice. There is a long story about him. There are stories to be told about everything and everybody in the town. Nowhere else do such wonderful things happen.

He was a peasant boy, little Petter Nord. He was short and round; he was brown-eyed and smiling. His hair was paler than birch leaves in the autumn; his cheeks were red and downy. And he was from Värmland. No one, seeing him, could imagine that he was from any other place. His native land had equipped him with its excellent qualities. He was quick at his work, nimble with his fingers, ready with his tongue, clear in his thoughts. And, moreover, full of fun, good-natured and brave, kind and quarrelsome, inquisitive and a chatterbox. A madcap, he never could show more respect to a burgomaster than to a beggar! But he had a heart; he fell in love every other day, and confided in the whole town.

This child of rich gifts attended to the work in the shop in rather an extraordinary manner. The customers were waited on while he fed the white mice. Money was changed and counted while he put wheels on his little automatic wagons. And while he told the customers of his very last love-affair, he kept his eye on the quart measure, into which the brown molasses was slowly curling. It delighted his admiring listeners to see him suddenly leap over the counter and rush out into the street to have a brush with a passing street-boy; also to see him calmly return to tie the string on a package or to finish measuring a piece of cloth.

Was it not quite natural that he should be the favorite of the whole town? We all felt obliged to trade with Halfvorson, after Petter Nord came there. Even the old Mayor himself was proud when Petter Nord took him apart into a dark corner and showed him the cages of the white mice. It was nervous work to show the mice, for Halfvorson had forbidden him to have them in the shop.

But then in the brightening February there came a few days of warm, misty weather. Petter Nord became suddenly serious and silent. He let the white mice nibble the steel bars of their cages without feeding them. He attended to his duties in the most irreproachable way. He fought with no more street boys. Could Petter Nord not bear the change in the weather?

Oh no, the matter was that he had found a fifty-crown note on one of the shelves. He believed that it had got caught in a piece of cloth, and without anyone's seeing him he had pushed it under a roll of striped cotton which was out of fashion and was never taken down from the shelf.

The boy was cherishing great anger in his heart against Halfvorson. The latter had destroyed a, whole family of mice for him, and now he meant to be revenged. Before his eyes he still saw the white mother with her helpless offspring. She had not made the slightest attempt to escape;

she had remained in her place with steadfast heroism, staring with red, burning eyes on the heartless murderer. Did he not deserve a short time of anxiety? Petter Nord wished to see him come out pale as death from his office and begin to look for the fifty crowns. He wished to see the same despair in his watery eyes as he had seen in the ruby red ones of the white mouse. The shopkeeper should search, he should turn the whole shop upside down before Petter Nord would let him find the bank-note.

But the fifty crowns lay in its hiding place all day without anyone's asking about it. It was a new note, many-colored and bright, and had big numbers in all the corners. When Petter Nord was alone in the shop, he put a step-ladder against the shelves and climbed up to the roll of cotton. Then he took out the fifty crowns, unfolded it and admired its beauties.

In the midst of the most eager trade he would grow anxious lest something should have happened to the fifty crowns. Then he pretended to look for something on the shelf, and groped about under the roll of cotton till he felt the smooth bank-note rustle under his fingers.

The note had suddenly acquired a supernatural power over him. Might there not be something living in it? The figures surrounded by wide rings were like magnetic eyes. The boy kissed them all and whispered: "I should like to have many, very many like you."

He began to have all sorts of thoughts about the note, and why Halfvorson did not inquire for it. Perhaps it was not Halfvorson's? Perhaps it had lain in the shop for a long time? Perhaps it no longer had any owner?

Thoughts are contagious. – At supper Halfvorson had begun to speak of money and moneyed-men. He told Petter Nord about all the poor boys who had amassed riches. He began with Whittington and ended with Astor and Jay Gould. Halfvorson knew all their histories; he knew how they had striven and denied themselves; what they had discovered and ventured. He grew eloquent when he began on such tales. He lived through the sufferings of those young people, he followed them in their successes; he rejoiced in their victories. Petter Nord listened quite fascinated.

Halfvorson was stone deaf, but that was no obstacle to conversation, for he read by the lips everything that was said. On the other hand, he could not hear his own voice. It rolled out as strangely monotonous as the roar of a distant waterfall. But his peculiar way of speaking made everything he said sink in, so that one could not escape from it for many days. Poor Petter Nord!

"What is most needed to become rich," said Halfvorson, "is the foundation. But it cannot be earned. Take note that they all have found it in the street or discovered it between the lining and cloth of a coat which they had bought at a pawnbroker's sale; or that it had been won at cards, or had been given to them in alms by a beautiful and charitable lady. After they had once found that blessed coin, everything had gone well with them. The stream of gold welled from it as from a fountain. The first thing that is necessary, Petter Nord, is the foundation."

Halfvorson's voice sounded ever fainter and fainter. Young Petter Nord sat in a kind of trance and saw endless vistas of gold before him. On the dining table rose great piles of ducats; the floor heaved white with silver, and the indistinct patterns on the dirty wall-paper changed into banknotes, big as handkerchiefs. But directly before his eyes fluttered the fifty-crown note, surrounded by wide rings, luring him like the most beautiful eyes. "Who can know," smiled the eyes, "perhaps the fifty crowns up on the shelf is just such a foundation?"

"Mark my words," said Halfvorson, "that, after the foundation, two things are necessary for those who wish to reach the heights. Work, untiring work, Petter Nord, is one; and the other is renunciation. Renunciation of play and love, of talk and laughter, of morning sleep and evening strolls. In truth, in truth, two things are necessary for him who would win fortune. One is called work, and the other renunciation."

Petter Nord looked as if he would like to weep. Of course he wished to be rich, naturally he wished to be fortunate, but fortune should not be so anxiously and sadly won. Fortune ought to come of herself. Just as Petter Nord was fighting with the street boys, the noble lady should stop her coach at the shop-door, and invite the Värmland boy to the place at her side. But now Halfvorson's voice still rolled in his ears. His brain was full of it. He thought of nothing else, knew nothing else. Work and renunciation, work and renunciation, that was life and the object of life. He asked nothing else, dared not think that he had ever wished anything else.

The next day he did not dare to kiss the fifty-crown note, did not dare even to look at it. He was silent and low-spirited, orderly and industrious. He attended to all his duties so irreproachably that anyone could see that there was something wrong with him. The old Mayor was troubled about the boy and did what he could to cheer him.

"Did you think of going to the Mid-Lent ball this evening?" asked the old man. "So, you did not. Well, then I invite you. And be sure that you come, or I will tell Halfvorson where you keep your mouse-cages."

Petter Nord sighed and promised to go to the ball.

The Mid-Lent ball, fancy Petter Nord at the Mid-Lent ball! Petter Nord would see all the beautiful ladies of the town, delicate, dressed in white, adorned with flowers. But of course Petter Nord would not be allowed to dance with a single one of them. Well, it did not matter. He was not in the mood to dance.

At the ball he stood in a doorway and made no attempt to dance. Several people had asked him to take part, but he had been firm and said no. He could not dance any of those dances. Neither would any of those fine ladies be willing to dance with him. He was much too humble for them.

But as he stood there, his eyes began to kindle and shine, and he felt joy creeping through his I hubs. It came from the dance music; it came from the fragrance of the flowers; it came from all the beautiful faces about him. After a little while he was so sparklingly happy that, if joy had been fire, he would have been surrounded by bursting flames. And if love were it, as many say it is, it would have been the same. He was always in love with some pretty girl, but hitherto with only one at a time. But when he now saw all those beautiful ladies together, it was no longer a single fire, which laid waste his sixteen-year-old heart; it was a whole conflagration.

Sometimes he looked down at his boots, which were by no means dancing shoes. But how he could have marked the time with the broad heels and spun round on the thick soles! Something was dragging and pulling him and trying to hurl him out on the floor like a whipped ball. He could still resist it, although his excitement grew stronger as the hours advanced. He grew delirious and hot. Heigh ho, he was no longer poor Petter Nord! He was the young whirlwind, that raises the seas and overthrows the forests.

Just then a hambo-polska* struck up. The peasant boy was quite beside himself. He thought it sounded like the polska, like the Värmland polska.

Suddenly Petter Nord was out on the floor. All his fine manners dropped off him. He was no longer at the town-hall ball; he was at home in the barn at the midsummer dance. He came forward, his knees bent, his head drawn down between his shoulders. Without stopping to ask, he threw his arms round a lady's waist and drew her with him. And then he began to dance the polska.

The girl followed him, half unwillingly, almost dragged. She was not in time; she did not know what kind of a dance it was, but suddenly it went quite of itself. The mystery of the dance was revealed to her. The

---

* A Swedish national dance of a very lively character

polska bore her, lifted her; her feet had wings; she felt as light as air. She thought that she was flying.

For the Värmland polska is the most wonderful dance. It transforms the heavy-footed sons of earth. Without a sound soles an inch thick float over the unplaned barn floor. They whirl about, light as leaves in an autumn wind. It is supple, quick, silent, gliding. Its noble, measured movements set the body free and let it feel itself light, elastic, floating.

While Petter Nord danced the dance of his native land, there was silence in the ballroom. At first people laughed, but then they all recognized that this was dancing. It floated away in even, rapid whirls; it was dancing indeed, if anything.

In the midst of his delirium Petter Nord perceived that round about him reigned a strange silence. He stopped short and passed his hand over his forehead. There was no black barn floor, no leafy walls, no light blue summer night, no merry peasant maiden in the reality he gazed upon. He was ashamed and wished to steal away.

But he was already surrounded, besieged. The young ladies crowded about the shop-boy and cried: "Dance with us; dance with us!"

They wished to learn the polska. They all wished to learn to dance the polska. The ball was turned from its course and became a dancing-school. All said that they had never known before what it was to dance. And Petter Nord was a great man for that evening. He had to dance with all the fine ladies, and they were exceedingly kind to him. He was only a boy, and such a madcap besides. No one could help making a pet of him.

Petter Nord felt that this was happiness. To be the favorite of the ladies, to dare to talk to them, to be in the midst of lights, of movement, to be made much of, to be petted, surely this was happiness.

When the ball was over, he was too happy to think about it. He needed to come home to be able to think over quietly what had happened to him that evening.

Halfvorson was not married, but he had in his house a niece who worked in the office. She was poor and dependent on Halfvorson, but she was quite haughty towards both him and Petter Nord. She had many friends among the more important people of the town and was invited to families where Halfvorson could never come. She and Petter Nord went home from the ball together.

"Do you know, Nord," asked Edith Halfvorson, "that a suit is soon to be brought against Halfvorson for illicit trading in brandy? You might tell me how it really is."

"There is nothing worth making a fuss about," said Petter Nord.

Edith sighed. "Of course there is nothing. But there will be a lawsuit and fines and shame without end. I wish that I really knew how it is."

"Perhaps it is best not to know anything," said Petter Nord.

"I wish to rise in the world, do you see," continued Edith, "and I wish to drag Halfvorson up with me, but he always drops back again. And then he does something so that I become impossible too. He is scheming something now. Do you not know what it is? It would be good to know."

"No," said Petter Nord, and not another word would he say. It was inhuman to talk to him of such things on the way home from his first ball.

Beyond the shop there was a little dark room for the shop-boy. There sat Petter Nord of today and came to an understanding with Petter Nord of yesterday. How pale and cowardly the churl looked. Now he heard what he really was. A thief and a miser. Did he know the seventh commandment? By rights he ought to have forty stripes. That was what he deserved.

God be blessed and praised for having let him go to the ball and get a new view of it all. Usch! what ugly thoughts he had had; but now it was quite changed. As if riches were worth sacrificing conscience and the soul's freedom for their sake! As if they were worth as much as a white mouse, if the heart could not be glad at the same time! He clapped his hands and cried out in joy – that he was free, free, free! There was not even a longing to possess the fifty crowns in his heart. How good it was to be happy!

When he had gone to bed, he thought that he would show Halfvorson the fifty crowns early the next morning. Then he became uneasy that the tradesman might come into the shop before him the next morning, search for the note and find it. He might easily think that Petter Nord had hidden it to keep it. The thought gave him no peace. He tried to shake it off, but he could not succeed. He could not sleep. So he rose, crept into the shop and felt about till he found the fifty crowns. Then he fell asleep with the note under his pillow.

An hour later he awoke. A light shone sharply in his eyes; a hand was fumbling under his pillow and a rumbling voice was scolding and swearing.

Before the boy was really awake, Halfvorson had the note in his hand and showed it to the two women, who stood in the doorway to his room. "You see that I was right," said Halfvorson. "You see that it was well worth while for me to drag you up to bear witness against him! You see that he is a thief!"

"No, no, no," screamed poor Petter Nord. "I did not wish to steal. I only hid the note."

Halfvorson heard nothing. Both the women stood with their backs turned to the room, as if determined to neither hear nor see.

Petter Nord sat up in bed. He looked all of a sudden pitifully weak and small. His tears were streaming. He wailed aloud.

"Uncle," said Edith, "he is weeping."

"Let him weep," said Halfvorson, "let him weep!" And he walked forward and looked at the boy. "You can weep all you like," he said, "but that does not take me in."

"Oh, oh," cried Petter Nord, "I am no thief. I hid the note as a joke – to make you angry. I wanted to pay you back for the mice. I am not a thief. Will no one listen to me. I am not a thief."

"Uncle," said Edith, "if you have tortured him enough now, perhaps we may go back to bed?"

"I know, of course, that it sounds terrible," said Halfvorson, "but it cannot be helped." He was gay, in very high spirits. "I have had my eye on you for a long time," he said to the boy. "You have always something you are tucking away when I come into the shop. But now I have caught you. Now I leave witnesses, and now I am going for the police."

The boy gave a piercing scream. "Will no one help me, will no one help me?" he cried. Halfvorson was gone, and the old woman who managed his house came up to him.

"Get up and dress yourself, Petter Nord! Halforson has gone for the police, and while he is away you can escape. The young lady can go out into the kitchen and get you a little food. I will pack your things."

The terrible weeping instantly ceased. After a short tine of hurry the boy was ready. He kissed both the women on the hand, humbly, like a whipped dog. And then off he ran.

They stood in the door and looked after him. When he was gone, they drew a sigh of relief.

"What will Halfvorson say?" said Edith.

"He will be glad," answered the housekeeper.

"He put the money there for the boy, I think. I guess that he wanted to be rid of him."

"But why? The boy was the best one we have had in the shop for many years."

"He probably did not want him to give testimony in the affair with the brandy."

Edith stood silent and breathed quickly. "It is so base, so base," she murmured. She clenched her fist towards the office and towards the little pane in the door, through which Halfvorson could see into the shop. She would have liked, she too, to have fled out into the world, away from all this meanness. She heard a sound far in, in the shop. She listened, went nearer, followed the noise, and at last found behind a keg of herring the cage of Petter Nord's white mice.

She took it up, put it on the counter, and opened the cage door. Mouse after mouse scampered out and disappeared behind boxes and barrels.

"May you flourish and increase," said Edith. "May you do injury and revenge your master!"

II

The little town lay friendly and contented under its red hill. It was so embedded in green that the church tower only just stuck up out of it. Garden after garden crowded one another on narrow terraces up the slope, and when they could go no further in that direction, they leaped with their bushes and trees across the street and spread themselves out between the scattered farmhouses and on the narrow strips of earth about them, until they were stopped by the broad river.

Complete silence and quiet reigned in the town. Not a soul was to be seen; only trees and bushes, and now and again a house. The only sound to be heard was the rolling of balls in the bowling-alley, like distant thunder on a summer day. It belonged to the silence.

But now the uneven stones of the marketplace were ground under iron-shod heels. The noise of coarse voices thundered against the walls of the town-hall and the church was thrown back from the mountain, and hastened unchecked down the long street. Four wayfarers disturbed the noonday peace.

Alas, for the sweet silence, the holiday peace of years! How terrified they were! One could almost see them betaking themselves in flight up the mountain slopes.

One of the noisy crew who broke into the village was Petter Nord, the Värmland boy, who six years before had run away, accused of theft. Those who were with him were three longshoremen from the big commercial town that lies only a few miles away.

How had little Petter Nord been getting on? He had been getting on well. He had found one of the most sensible of friends and companions.

As he ran away from the village in the dark, rainy February morning, the polska tunes seethed and roared in his ears. And one of them was more persistent than all the others. It was the one they all had sung during the ring dance.

Christmas time has come,
Christmas time has come,
And after Christmas time comes Easter.
That is not true at all,
That is not true at all,
For Lent comes after Christmas feasting.

The fugitive heard it so distinctly, so distinctly. And then the wisdom that is hidden in the old ring dance forced itself upon the little pleasure-loving Värmland boy, forced itself into his very fiber, blended with every drop of blood, soaked into his brain and marrow. It is so; that is the meaning. Between Christmas and Easter, between the festivals of birth and death, comes life's fasting. One shall ask nothing of life; it is a poor, miserable fast. One shall never trust it, however it may appear. The next moment it is grey and ugly again. It is not its fault, poor thing, it cannot help it!

Petter Nord felt almost proud at having cheated life out of its most profound secret.

He thought he saw the pallid Spirit of Fasting creeping about over the earth in the shape of a beggar with Lenten twigs* in her hand. And he heard how she hissed at him: "You have wished to celebrate the festival of joy and merry moods in the midst of the time of fasting, which is called life. Therefore shame and dishonor shall befall you, until you change your ways."

He had changed his ways, and the Spirit of Fasting had protected him. He had never needed to go farther than to the big town, for he was never followed. And in its working quarter the Spirit of Fasting had her dwelling. Petter Nord found work in a machine shop. He grew strong and energetic. He became serious and thrifty. He had fine Sunday clothes; he acquired new knowledge, borrowed books and went to lectures. There was nothing really left of little Petter Nord but his white hair and his brown eyes.

That night had broken something in him, and the heavy work at the machine-shop made the break ever bigger, so that the wild Värmland

* Translator's Note: In Sweden, just before Easter, bunches of birch twigs with small feathers tied on the ends, are sold everywhere on the streets. The origin of this custom is unknown.

boy had crept quite out through it. He no longer talked nonsense, for no one was allowed to speak in the shop, and he soon learned silent ways. He no longer invented anything new, for since he had to look after springs and wheels in earnest, he no longer found them amusing. He never fell in love, for he could not be interested in the women of the working quarter, after he had learned to know the beauties of his native town. He had no mice, no squirrels, nothing to play with. He had no time; he understood that such things were useless, and he thought with horror of the time when he used to fight with street boys.

Petter Nord did not believe that life could be anything but grey, grey, grey. Petter Nord always had a dull time, but he was so used to it that he did not notice it. Petter Nord was proud of himself because he had become so virtuous. He dated his good behavior from that night when Joy failed him and Fasting became his companion and friend.

But how could the virtuous Petter Nord be coming to the village on a work-day, accompanied by three boon companions, who were loafers and drunken?

He had always been a good boy, poor Petter Nord. And he had always tried to help those three good-for-nothings as well as he could, although he despised them. He had come with wood to their miserable hovel, when the winter was most severe, and he had patched and mended their clothes. The men held together like brothers, principally because they were all three named Petter. That name united them much more than if they bad been born brothers. And now they allowed the boy on account of that name to do them friendly services, and when they had got their grog ready and settled themselves comfortably on their wooden chairs, they entertained him, sitting and darning the gaping holes in their stockings, with gallows humor and adventurous lies. Petter Nord liked it, although he would not acknowledge it. They were now for him almost what the mice had been formerly.

Now it happened that these wharf-rats had heard some gossip from the village. And after the space of six years they brought Petter Nord information that Halfvorson had put the fifty crowns out for him to disqualify him as a witness. And in their opinion Petter Nord ought to go back to the town and punish Halfvorson.

But Petter Nord was sensible and deliberate, and equipped with the wisdom of this world. He would not have anything to do with such a proposal.

The Petters spread the story about through the whole quarter. Everyone said to Petter Nord: "Go back and punish Halfvorson, then you will be arrested, and there will be a trial, and the thing will get into the papers, and the fellow's shame will be known throughout all the land."

But Petter Nord would not. It might be amusing, but revenge is a costly pleasure, and Petter Nord knew that Life is poor. Life cannot afford such amusements.

One morning the three men had come to him and said that they were going in his place to beat Halfvorson, "that justice should be done on earth," as they said.

Petter Nord threatened to kill all three of them if they went one step on the way to the village.

Then one of them who was little and short, and whose name was Long-Petter, made a speech to Petter Nord.

"This earth," he said, "is an apple hanging by a string over a fire to roast. By the fire I mean the kingdom of the evil one; Petter Nord, and the apple must hang near the fire to be sweet and tender; but if the string breaks and the apple falls into the fire, it is destroyed. Therefore the string is very important, Petter Nord. Do you understand what is meant by the string?"

"I guess it must be a steel wire," said Petter Nord.

"By the string I mean justice," said Long-Petter with deep seriousness. "If there is no justice on earth, everything falls into the fire. Therefore the avenger may not refuse to punish, or if he will not do it, others must."

"This is the last time I will offer any of you any grog," said Petter Nord, quite unmoved by the speech.

"Yes, it can't be helped," said Long-Petter, "justice must be done."

"We do not do it to be thanked by you, but in order that the honorable name of Petter shall not be brought to disrepute," said one, whose name was Rulle-Petter, and who was tall and morose.

"Really, is the name so highly esteemed!" said Petter Nord, contemptuously.

"Yes, and the worst of it is that they are beginning to say everywhere in all the saloons that you must have meant to steal the fifty crowns, since you will not have the shopkeeper punished."

Those words bit in deep. Petter Nord started up and said that he would go and beat the shopkeeper.

"Yes, and we will go with you and help you," said the loafers.

And so they started off, four men strong, to the village. At first Petter Nord was gloomy and surly, and much more angry with his friends than with his enemy. But when he came to the bridge over the river, he became quite changed. He felt as if he had met there a little, weeping fugitive, and had crept into him. And as he became more at home in the old Petter Nord he felt what a grievous wrong the shopkeeper had done him. Not only because he had tried to tempt him and ruin him, but, worst of all, because he had driven him away from that town, where Petter Nord could have remained Petter Nord all the days of his life. Oh, what fun he had had in those days, how happy and glad he had been, how open his heart, how beautiful the world! Lord God, if he had only been allowed always to live here! And he thought of what he was now – silent and stupid, serious and industrious – quite like a prodigal.

He grew passionately angry with Halfvorson, and instead of, as before, following his companions, he dashed past them.

But the tramps, who had not come merely to punish Halfvorson, but also to let their wrath break loose, hardly knew how to begin. There was nothing for an angry man to do here. There was not a dog to chase, not a street-sweeper to pick a quarrel with, nor a fine gentleman at whom to throw an insult.

It was early in the year; the spring was just turning into summer. It was the white time of cherry and hawthorn blossoms, when bunches of lilacs cover the high, round bushes, and the air is full of the fragrance of the apple-blossoms. These men who had come direct from paved streets and wharves to this realm of flowers were strangely affected by it. Three pairs of fists that till now had been fiercely clenched, relaxed, and three pairs of heels thundered a little less violently against the pavement.

From the marketplace they saw a pathway that wound up the hill. Along it grew young cherry trees which formed vaulted arches with their white tops. The arch was light and floating, and the branches absurdly slender, altogether weak, delicate and youthful.

The cherry tree path attracted the eyes of the men against their will. What an unpractical hole it was, where people planted cherry trees, where anyone could take the cherries. The three Petters had considered it before as a nest of iniquity, full of cruelty and tyranny. Now they began to laugh at it, and even to despise it a little.

But the fourth one of the company did not laugh. His longing for revenge was seething ever more fiercely, for he felt that this was the town where he ought to have lived and labored. It was his lost paradise. And without paying any attention to the others he walked quickly up the street.

They followed him; and when they saw that there was only one street, and when they saw only flowers, and more flowers the whole length of it, their scorn and their good humor increased. It was perhaps the first time in their lives that they had ever noticed flowers, but here they could not help it, for the clusters of lilac blossoms brushed off their caps and the petals of cherry-blossoms rained down over them.

"What kind of people do you suppose live in this town?" said Long-Petter, musingly.

"Bees," answered Cobbler-Petter, who had received his name because he had once lived in the same house as a shoemaker.

Of course, little by little, they perceived a few people. In the windows, behind shining panes and white curtains, appeared young, pretty faces, and they saw children playing on the terraces. But no noise disturbed the silence. It seemed to them as if the trump of the Day of Doom itself would not be able to wake this town. What could they do with themselves in such a town!

They went into a shop and bought some beer. There they asked several questions of the shopman in a terrible voice. They asked if the fire-brigade had their engines in order, and wondered if there were clappers in the church bells, if there should happen to be an alarm.

They drank their beer in the street and threw the bottles away. One, two, three, all the bottles at the same corner, thunder and crash, and the splinters flew about their ears.

They heard steps behind them, real steps; voices, loud, distinct voices; laughter, much laughter, and, moreover, a rattling as if of metal. They were appalled, and drew back into a doorway. It sounded like a whole company.

It was one, too, but of young girls. All the maids of the town were going out in a body to the pastures to milk.

It made the deepest impression on these city men, these citizens of the world. The maids of the town with milk-pails! It was almost touching!

They suddenly jumped out of their doorway and cried "Boo!"

The whole troop of girls scattered instantly. They screamed and ran. Their skirts fluttered; their head cloths loosened; their milk-pails rolled about the street.

And at the same time, along the whole street, was heard a deafening sound of gates and doors slammed to, of hooks and bolts and locks.

Farther down the street stood a big linden tree, and under it sat an old woman by a table with candies and cakes. She did not move; she did not look round; she only sat still. She was not asleep either.

"She is made of wood," said Cobbler-Petter.

"No, of clay," said Rulle-Petter.

They walked abreast, all three. Just in front of the old woman they began to reel. They staggered against her table. And the old woman began to scold.

"Neither of wood nor of clay," they said, – "venom, only venom."

During all this time Petter Nord had not spoken to them, but now, at last, they were directly in front of Halfvorson's shop, and there he was waiting for them.

"This is undeniably, my affair," he said proudly, and pointed at the shop. "I wish to go in alone and attend to it. If I do not succeed, then you may try."

They nodded. "Go ahead, Petter Nord! We will wait outside."

Petter Nord went in, found a young man alone in the shop, and asked about Halfvorson. He heard that the latter had gone away. He had quite a talk with the clerk, and obtained a good deal of information about his master.

Halfvorson had never been accused of illicit trade. How he had behaved towards Petter Nord everyone knew, but no one spoke of that affair anymore. Halfvorson had risen in the world, and now he was not at all dangerous. He was not inhuman to his debtors, and had ceased to spy on his shop-boys. The last few years he had devoted himself to gardening. He had laid out a garden around his house in the town, and a kitchen garden near the customhouse. He worked so eagerly in his gardens that he scarcely thought of amassing money.

Petter Nord felt a stab in his heart. Of course the man was good. He had remained in paradise. Of course anyone was good who lived there.

Edith Halfvorson was still with her uncle, but she had been ill for a while. Her lungs were weak, ever since an attack of pneumonia in the winter.

While Petter Nord was listening to all this, and more too, the three men stood outside and waited.

In Halfvorson's shadeless garden a bower of birch had been arranged so that Edith might lie there in the beautiful, warm spring days. She regained her strength slowly, but her life was no longer in danger.

Some people make one feel that they are not able to live. At their first illness they lie down and die. Halfvorson's niece was long since weary of everything, of the office, of the dim little shop, of money-getting. When she was seventeen years old, she had the incentive of winning friends and acquaintances. Then she undertook to try to keep Halfvorson in the path of virtue, but now everything was accomplished. She saw no prospect of escaping from the monotony of her life. She might as well die.

She was of an elastic nature, like a steel spring: a bundle of nerves and vivacity, when anything troubled or tormented her. How she had worked with strategy and artifice, with womanly goodness and womanly daring, before she had reached the point with her uncle when she was sure that there was no longer danger of any Petter Nord affairs! But now that he was tamed and subdued, she had nothing to interest her. Yes, and yet she would not die! She lay and thought of what she would do when she was well again.

Suddenly she started up, hearing someone say in a very loud voice that he alone wished to settle with Halvorson. And then another voice answered: "Go ahead, Petter Nord!"

Petter Nord was the most terrible, the most fatal name in the world. It meant a revival of all the old troubles. Edith rose with trembling limbs, and just then three dreadful creatures came around the corner and stopped to stare at her. There was only a low rail and a thin hedge between her and the street.

Edith was alone. The maids had gone to milk, and Halfvorson was working in his garden by the custom-house, although he had told the shop-boy to nay that he had gone away, for he was ashamed of his passion for gardening. Edith was terribly frightened at the three men as well as at the one who had gone into the shop. She was sure that they wished to do her harm. So she turned and ran up the mountain by the steep, slippery path and the narrow, rotten wooden steps which led from terrace to terrace.

The strange men thought it too delightfully funny that she ran from them. They could not resist pretending that they wished to catch her. One of them climbed up on the railing, and all three shouted with a terrible voice.

Edith ran as one runs in dreams, panting, falling, terrified to death, with a horrible feeling of not getting away from one spot. All sorts of emotions stormed through her, and shook her so that she thought she was going to die. Yes, if one of those men laid his hand on her, she knew that she should die. When she had reached the highest terrace, and dared to look back, she found that the men were still in the street, and were no longer looking at her. Then she threw herself down on the ground, quite powerless. The exertion had been greater than she could bear. She felt something burst in her. Then blood streamed from her lips.

She was found by the maids as they went home from the milking. She was then half dead. For the moment she was brought back to life, but no one dared to hope that she could live long.

She could not talk that day enough to tell in what way she had been frightened. Had she done so, it is uncertain if the strange men had come alive from the town. They fared badly enough as it was. For after Petter Nord had come out to them again, and had told them that Halfvorson was not at home, all four of them in good accord went out through the gates, and found a sunny slope where they could sleep away the time until the shopman returned.

But in the afternoon, when all the men of the town, who had been working in the fields, came home again, the women told them about the tramps' visit, about their threatening questions in the shop where they had bought the beer, and about all their boisterous behavior. The women exaggerated and magnified everything, for they had sat at home and frightened one another the whole afternoon. Their husbands believed that their houses and homes were in danger. They determined to capture the disturbers of the peace, found a stout-hearted man to lead them, took thick cudgels with them and started off.

The whole town was alive. The women came out on their doorsteps and frightened one another. It was both terrible and exciting.

Before long the captors returned with their game. They had them all four. They had made a ring round them while they slept and captured them. No heroism had been required for the deed.

Now they came back to the town with them, driving them as if they had been animals. A mad thirst for revenge had seized upon the conquerors. They struck for the pleasure of striking. When one of the prisoners clenched his fist at them, he received a blow on the head which knocked him down, and thereupon blows hailed upon him, until he got up and went on. The four men were almost dead.

The old poems are so beautiful. The captured hero sometimes must walk in chains in the triumphal procession of his victorious enemy. But he is proud and beautiful still in adversity. And looks follow him as well as the fortunate one who has conquered him. Beauty's tears and wreaths belong to him still, even in misfortune.

But who could be enraptured of poor Petter Nord? His coat was torn and his tow-colored hair sticky with blood. He received the most blows, for he offered the most resistance. He looked terrible, as he walked. He roared without knowing it. Boys caught hold of him, and he dragged them long distances. Once he stopped and flung off the crowd in the street. Just as he was about to escape, a blow from a cudgel fell on his head and knocked him down. He rose up again, half stunned, and staggered on, blows raining upon him, and the boys hanging like leeches to his arms and legs.

They met the old Mayor, who was on his way home from his game of whist in the garden of the inn. "Yes," he said to the advance guard, – "yes, take them to the prison."

He placed himself at the head of the procession, shouted and ordered. In a second everything was in line. Prisoners and guards marched in peace and order. The villagers' cheeks flushed; some of them threw down their cudgels; others put them on their shoulders like muskets. And so the prisoners were transferred into the keeping of the police, and were taken to the prison in the marketplace.

Those who had saved the town stood a long time in the marketplace and told of their courage and of their great exploit. And in the little room of the inn, where the smoke is as thick as a cloud, and the great men of the town mix their midnight toddy, more is heard of the deed, magnified. They grow bigger in their rocking-chairs; they swell in their sofa corners; they are all heroes. What force is slumbering in that little town of mighty memories! Thou formidable inheritance, thou old Viking blood!

The old Mayor did not like the whole affair. He could not quite reconcile himself to the stirring of the old Viking blood. He could not sleep for thinking of it, and went out again into the street and strolled slowly towards the square.

It was a mild spring night. The church clock's only hand pointed to eleven. The balls had ceased to roll on the bowling alley. The curtains were drawn down. The houses seemed to sleep with closed eyelids. The steep hill behind was black, as if in mourning. But in the midst of all the sleep there was one thing awake – the fragrance of the flowers did not sleep. It stole over the linden hedges; poured out from the gardens; rushed up and down the street; climbed up to every window standing open, to every skylight that sucked in fresh air.

Everyone whom the fragrance reached instantly saw before him his little town, although the darkness had gently settled down over it. He saw it as a village of flowers, where it was not house by house, but garden by garden. He saw the cherry trees that raised their white arches over the steep wood-path, the lilac clusters, the swelling buds of glorious roses, the proud peonies, and the drifts of flower-petals on the ground beneath the hawthorns.

The old Mayor was deep in thought. He was so wise and so old. Seventy years had he reached, and for fifty he had managed the affairs of the town. But that night be asked himself if he had done right. "I had the town in my hand," he thought, "but I have not made it anything great." And he thought of its great past, and was the more uncertain if he had done right.

He stood in the marketplace, looking out over the river. A boat came with oars. A few villagers were coming home from a picnic. Girls in light dresses held the oars. They steered in under the arch of the bridge, but there the current was strong and they were drawn back. There was a violent struggle. Their slender bodies were bent backwards, until they lay even with the edge of the boat. Their soft arm-muscles tightened. The oars bent like bows. The noise of laughter and cries filled the air.

Again and again the current conquered. The boat was driven back. And when at last the girls had to land at the market quay, and leave the boat for men to take home, how red and vexed they were, and how they laughed! How their laughter echoed down the street! How their broad, shady hats, their light, fluttering summer dresses enlivened the quiet night.

The old Mayor saw in his mind's eye, for in the darkness he could not see them distinctly, their sweet, young faces, their beautiful clear eyes and red lips. Then he straightened himself proudly up. The little town was not without all glory. Other communities could boast of other things, but he knew no place richer in flowers and in the enchanting fairness of its women.

Then the old man thought with newborn courage of his efforts. He need not fear for the future of the town. Such a town did not need to protect itself with strict laws.

He felt compassion on the unfortunate prisoners. He went and waked the justice of the peace, and talked with him. And the two were of one mind. They went together to the prison and set Petter Nord and his companions free.

And they did right. For the little town is like the Milo Aphrodite. It has alluring beauty, and it lacks arms to hold fast.

III

I shall almost be compelled to leave reality, and turn to the world of saga and extravagance to be able to relate what now happened. If young Petter Nord had been Per, the Swineherd, with a gold crown under his hat, it would all have seemed simple and natural. But no one, of course, will believe me if I say that Petter Nord also wore a royal crown on his tow hair. No one can ever know how many wonderful things happen in that little town. No one can guess how many enchanted princesses are waiting there for the shepherd boy of adventure.

At first it looked as if there were to be no more adventures. For when Petter Nord had been set free by the old Mayor, and for the second time had to flee in shame and disgrace from the town, the same thoughts came over him as when he fled the first time. The polska tunes rang again suddenly in his ears, and loudest among them all sounded the old ring-dance.

Christmas time has come,
Christmas time has come,
And after Christmas time comes Easter.
That is not true at all,
That is not true at all,
For Lent comes after Christmas feasting.

And he saw distinctly the pallid Spirit of Fasting stealing about over the earth with her bundle of twigs on her arm. And she called to him: "Spendthrift, spendthrift! You have wished to celebrate the festival of revenge and reparation during the time of fasting, that is called life. Can you afford such extravagances, foolish one?"

Thereupon he had again sworn obedience and become the quiet and thrifty workman. He again stood peaceful and sensible at his work. No one could believe that it was he who had roared with rage and flung about the people in the street, as an elk at bay shakes off the dogs.

A few weeks later Halfvorson came to him at the machine-shop. He looked him up, at his niece's desire. She wished, if possible, to speak to him that same day.

Petter Nord began to shake and tremble when he saw Halfvorson. It was as if he had seen a slippery snake. He did not know which he wished most – to strike him or to run away from him; but he soon perceived that Halfvorson looked much troubled.

The tradesman looked as one does after having been out in a strong wind. The muscles of his face were drawn; his mouth was compressed; his eyes red and full of tears. He struggled visibly with some sorrow. The only thing in him that was the same was his voice. It was as inhumanly expressionless as ever.

"You need not be afraid of the old story nor of the new one either," said Halfvorson. "It is known that you were with those men who made all the trouble with us the other day. And as we supposed that they came from here, I could learn where you were. Edith is going to die soon," he continued, and his whole face twitched as if it would fall to pieces. "She wishes to speak to you before she dies. But we wish you no harm."

"Of course I shall come," said Petter Nord.

Soon they were both on board the steamer. Petter Nord was decked out in his fine Sunday clothes. Under his hat played and smiled all the dreams of his boyhood in a veritable kingly crown; they encircled his light hair. Edith's message made him quite dizzy. Had he not always thought that fine ladies would love him? And now here was one who wished to see him before she died. Most wonderful of all things wonderful! – He sat and thought of her as she had been formerly. How proud, how alive! And now she was going to die. He was in such sorrow for her sake. But that she had been thinking of him all these years! A warm, sweet melancholy came over him.

He was really there again, the old, mad Petter Nord. As soon as he approached the village the Spirit of Fasting went away from him with disgust and contempt.

Halfvorson could not keep still for a moment. The heavy gale, which he alone perceived, swept him forward and back on the deck. As he passed Petter, he murmured a few words, so that the latter could know by what paths his despairing thoughts wandered.

"They found her on the ground, half dead – blood everywhere about her," he said once. And another time: "Was she not good? Was she not beautiful? How could such things come to her?" And again: "She has made me good too. Could not see her sitting in sorrow all day long and ruining the account-book with her tears." Then this came: "A clever child, besides. Won her way with me. Made my home pleasant. Got me acquaintances among fine people. Understood what she was after, but could not resist her." He wandered away to the bow of the boat. When he came back he said: "I cannot bear to have her die."

He said it all with that helpless voice, which he could not subdue or control. Petter Nord had a proud feeling that such a man as he who wore a royal crown on his brow had no right to be angry with Halfvorson. The latter was separated from men by his infirmity, and could not win their love. Therefore he had to treat them all as enemies. He was not to be measured by the same standard as other people.

Petter Nord sank again into his dreams. *She* had remembered him all these years, and now she could not die before she had seen him. Oh, fancy that a young girl for all these years had been thinking of him, loving him, missing him!

As soon as they landed and reached the tradesman's house, he was taken to Edith, who was waiting for him in the arbor.

The happy Petter Nord woke from his dreams when he saw her. She was a fair vision, this girl, withering away in emulation with the rootless birches around her. Her big eyes had darkened and grown clearer. Her hands were so thin and transparent that one feared to touch them for their fragility.

And it was she who loved him. Of course he had to love her instantly in return, deeply, dearly, ardently! It was bliss, after so many years, to feel his heart glow at the sight of a fellow-being.

He had stopped motionless at the entrance of the arbor, while eyes, heart and brain worked most eagerly. When she saw how he stood and stared at her, she began to smile with that most despairing smile in the world, the smile of the very ill, that says: "See, this is what I have become, but do not count on me! I cannot be beautiful and charming any longer. I must die soon."

It brought him back to reality. He saw that he had to do not with a vision, but with a spirit which was about to spread its wings, and therefore had made the walls of its prison so delicate and transparent. It now showed so plainly in his face and in the way he took Edith's hand, that he all at once suffered with her suffering, – that he had forgotten everything but grief, that she was going to die. The sick girl felt the same pity for herself, and her eyes filled with tears.

Oh, what sympathy he felt for her from the first moment. He understood instantly that she would not wish to show her emotion. Of course it was agitating for her to see him, whom she had longed for so long, but it was her weakness that had made her betray herself. She naturally would not like him to pay any attention to it. And so he began on an innocent subject of conversation.

"Do you know what happened to my white mice?" he said.

She looked at him with admiration. He seemed to wish to make the way easier for her. "I let them loose in the shop," she said. "They have thriven well."

"No, really! Are there any of them left?"

"Halfvorson says that he will never be rid of Petter Nord's mice. They have revenged you, you understand," she said with meaning.

"It was a very good race," answered Petter Nord, proudly.

The conversation lagged for a while. Edith closed her eyes, as if to rest, and he kept a respectful silence. His last answer she had not understood. He had not responded to what she had said about revenge. When he began to talk of the mice, she believed that he understood what she wished to say to him. She knew that he had come to the town a few weeks before to be revenged. Poor Petter Nord! Many a time she had wondered what had become of him. Many a night had the cries of the frightened boy come to her in dreams. It was partly for his sake that she should never again have to live through such a night, that she had begun to reform her uncle, had made his house a home for him, had let the lonely man feel the value of having a sympathetic friend near him. Her lot was now again bound together with that of Petter Nord. His attempt at revenge had frightened her to death. As soon as she had regained her strength after that severe attack, she had begged Halfvorson to look him up.

And Petter Nord sat there and believed that it was for love she had called him. He could not know that she believed him vindictive, coarse, degraded, a drunkard and a bully. He who was an example to all his comrades in the working quarter, he could not guess that she had summoned him, in order to preach virtue and good habits to him, in order to say to him, if nothing else helped: "Look at me, Petter Nord! It is your want of judgment, your vindictiveness, that is the cause of my death. Think of it, and begin another life!"

He had come filled with love of life and dreams to celebrate love's festival, and she lay there and thought of plunging him into the black depths of remorse.

There must have been something of the glory of the kingly crown shining on her, which made her hesitate so that she decided to question him first.

"But, Petter Nord, was it really you who were here with those three terrible men?"

He flushed and looked on the ground. Then he had to tell her the whole story of the day with all its shame. In the first place, what unmanliness he had shown in not sooner demanding justice, and how he had only gone because he was forced to it, and then how he had been beaten and whipped instead of beating someone himself. He did not dare to look up while he was speaking; he did expect that even those gentle eyes would judge him with forbearance. He felt that he was robbing himself of all the glory with which she must have surrounded him in her dreams.

"But Petter Nord, what would have happened if you had met Halfvorson?" asked Edith, when he had finished.

He hung his head even lower. "I saw him well enough," he said. "He had not gone away. He was working in his garden outside the gates. The boy in the shop told me everything."

"Well, why did you not avenge yourself?" said Edith.

He was spared nothing. – But he felt the inquiring glance of her eyes on him and he began obediently: "When the men lay down to sleep on a slope, I went alone to find Halfvorson, for I wished to have him to myself. He was working there, staking his peas. It must have rained in torrents the day before, for the peas had been broken down to the ground; some of the leaves were whipped to ribbons, others covered with earth. It was like a hospital, and Halfvorson was the doctor. He raised them up so gently, brushed away the earth and helped the poor little things to cling to the twigs. I stood and looked on. He did not hear me, and he had no time to look up. I tried to retain my anger by force. But what could I do? I could not fly at him while he was busy with the peas. My time will come afterwards, I thought.

"But then he started up, struck himself on the forehead and rushed away to the hotbed. He lifted the glass and looked in, and I looked too, for he seemed to be in the depths of despair. Yes, it was dreadful, of course. He had forgotten to shade it from the sun, and it must have been terribly hot under the glass. The cucumbers lay there half-dead and gasped for breath; some of the leaves were burned, and others were drooping. I was so overcome, I too, that I never thought what I was doing, and Halfvorson caught sight of my shadow. 'Look here, take the watering-pot that is standing in the asparagus bed and run down to the river for water,' he said, without looking up. I suppose he thought it was the gardener's boy. And I ran."

"Did you, Petter Nord?"

"Yes; you see, the cucumbers ought not to suffer on account of our enmity. I thought myself that it showed lack of character and so on, but I could not help it. I wanted to see if they would come to life. When I came back, he had lifted the glass off and still stood and stared despairingly. I thrust the watering-pot into his hand, and he began to pour over them. Yes, it was almost visible what good it did in the hotbed. I thought almost that they raised themselves, and he must have thought so too, for he began to laugh. Then I ran away."

"You ran away, Petter Nord, you ran away?"

Edith had raised herself in the armchair.

"I could not strike him," said Petter Nord.

Edith felt an ever stronger impression of the glory round poor Petter Nord's head. So it was not necessary to plunge him into the depths of remorse with the heavy burden of sin around his neck. Was he such a man? Such a tender-hearted, sensitive man! She sank back, closed her eyes and thought. She did not need to say it to him. She was astonished that she felt such a relief not to have to cause him pain.

"I am so glad that you have given up your plans for revenge, Petter Nord," she began in friendly tones. "It was about that that I wished to talk to you. Now I can die in peace."

He drew along breath. She was not unfriendly.

She did not look as if she had been mistaken in him. She must love him very much when she could excuse such cowardice. – For when she said that she had sent for him to ask him to give up his thoughts of revenge, it must have been from bashfulness not to have to acknowledge the real reason of the summons. She was so right in it. He who was the man ought to say the first word.

"How can they let you die?" he burst out.

"Halfvorson and all the others, how can they? If I were here, I would refuse to let you die. I would give you all my strength. I would take all your suffering."

"I have no pain," she said, smiling at such bold promises.

"I am thinking that I would like to carry you away like a frozen bird, lay you under my vest like a young squirrel. Fancy what it would be to work if something so warm and soft was waiting for one at home! But if you were well, there would be so many –"

She looked at him with weary surprise, prepared to put him back in his proper place. But she must have seen again something of the magic crown about the boy's head, for she had patience with him. He meant nothing. He had to talk as he did. He was not like others.

"Ah," she said, indifferently, "there are not so many, Petter Nord. There has hardly been anyone in earnest."

But now there came another turn to his advantage. In her suddenly awoke the eager hunger of a sick person for compassion. She longed for the tenderness, the pity that the poor workman could give her. She felt the need of being near that deep, disinterested sympathy. The sick cannot have enough of it. She wished to read it in his glance and his whole being. Words meant nothing to her.

"I like to see you here," she said. "Sit here for a while, and tell me what you have been doing these six years!"

While he talked, she lay and drew in the indescribable something which passed between them. She heard and yet she did not hear. But by some strange sympathy she felt herself strengthened and vivified.

Nevertheless she did get one impression from his story. It took her into the workman's quarter, into a new world, full of tumultuous hopes and strength. How they longed and trusted! How they hated and suffered!

"How happy the oppressed are," she said.

It occurred to her, with a longing for life, that there might be something for her there, she who always needed oppression and compulsion to make life worth living.

"If I were well," she said, "perhaps I would have gone there with you. I should enjoy working my way up with someone I liked."

Petter Nord started. Here was the confession that he had been waiting for the whole time. "Oh, can you not live!" he prayed. And he beamed with happiness.

She became observant. "That is love," she said to herself. "And now he believes that I am also in love. What madness, that Värmland boy!"

She wished to bring him back to reason, but there was something in Petter Nord on that day of victory that restrained her. She had not the heart to spoil his happy mood. She felt compassion for his foolishness and let him live in it. "It does not matter, as I am to die so soon," she said to herself.

But she sent him away soon after, and when he asked if he might not come again, she forbade him absolutely. "But," she said, "do you remember our graveyard up on the hill, Petter Nord. You can come there in a few weeks and thank death for that day."

As Petter Nord came out of the garden, he met Halfvorson. He was walking forward and back in despair, and his only consolation was the thought that Edith was laying the burden of remorse on the wrong-doer. To see him overpowered by pangs of conscience, for that alone had he sought him out. But when he met the young workman, he saw that Edith had not told him everything. He was serious, but at the same time he certainly was madly happy.

"Has Edith told you why she is dying?" said Halfvorson.

"No," answered Petter Nord.

Halfvorson laid his hand on his shoulder as if to keep him from escaping.

"She is dying because of you, because of your damned pranks. She was slightly ill before, but it was nothing. No one thought that she would die; but then you came with those three wretched tramps, and they frightened her while you were in my shop. They chased her, and she ran away from them, ran till she got a hemorrhage. But that is what you wanted; you wished to be revenged on me by killing her, wished to leave me lonely and unhappy without a soul near me who cares for me. All my joy you wished to take from me, all my joy."

He would have gone on forever, overwhelmed Petter Nord with reproaches, killed him with curses; but the latter tore himself away and ran, as if an earthquake had shaken the town and all the houses were tumbling down.

IV

Behind the town the mountain walls rise perpendicularly, but after one has climbed up them by steep stone steps and slippery pine paths, one finds that the mountain spreads out into a wide, undulating plateau. And there lies an enchanted wood.

Over the whole stretch of the mountain stands a pine wood without pine-needles; a wood which dies in the spring and grows green in the autumn; a lifeless wood, which blossoms with the joy of life when other trees are laying aside their green garments; a wood that grows without anyone knowing how, that stands green in winter frosts and brown in summer dews.

It is a newly-planted wood. Young firs have been forced to take root in the clefts between the granite blocks. Their tough roots have bored down like sharp wedges into the fissures and crevices. It was very well for a while; the young trees shot up like spires, and the roots bored down into the granite. But at last they could go no further, and then the wood was filled with an ill-concealed peevishness. It wished to go high, but also deep. After the way down had been closed to it, it felt that life was not worth living. Every spring it was ready to throw off the burden of life in its discouragement. During the summer when Edith was dying, the young wood was quite brown. High above the town of flowers stood a gloomy row of dying trees.

But up on the mountain it is not all gloom and the agony of death. As one walks between the brown trees, in such distress that one is ready to die, one catches glimpses of green trees. The perfume of flowers fills the air; the song of birds exults and calls. Then thoughts rise of the sleeping forest and of the paradise of the fairy-tale, encircled by thorny thickets. And when one comes at last to the green, to the flower fragrance, to the song of the birds, one sees that it is the hidden graveyard of the little town.

The home of the dead lies in an earth-filled hollow in the mountain plateau. And there, within the grey stone walls, the knowledge and weariness of life end. Lilacs stand at the entrance, bending under heavy clusters. Lindens and beeches spread a lofty arch of luxuriant growth over the whole place. Jasmines and roses blossom freely in that consecrated earth. Over the big old tombstones creep vines of ivy and periwinkle.

There is a corner where the pine trees grow mast-high. Does it not seem as if the young wood outside ought to be ashamed at the sight of them? And there are hedges there, quite grown beyond their keeper's hands, blooming and sending forth shoots without thought of shears or knife.

The town now has a new burial-place, to which the dead can come without special trouble. It was a weary way for them to be carried up in winter, when the steep wood-paths are covered with ice, and the steps slippery and covered with snow. The coffin creaked; the bearers panted;

the old clergyman leaned heavily on the sexton and the grave-digger. Now no one has to be buried up there who does not ask it.

The graves are not beautiful. There are few who know how to make the resting-place of the dead attractive. But the fresh green sheds its peace and beauty over them all. It is strangely solemn to know that those who are buried are glad to lie there. The living who go up after a day hot with work, go there as among friends. Those who sleep have also loved the lofty trees and the stillness.

If a stranger comes up there, they do not tell him of death and loss; they sit down on the big slabs of stone, on the broad burgomaster tombs, and tell him about Petter Nord, the Värmland boy, and of his love. The story seems fitting to be told up here, where death has lost its terrors. The consecrated earth seems to rejoice at having also been the scene of awakened happiness and newborn life.

For it happened that after Petter Nord ran away from Halfvorson, he sought refuge in the graveyard.

At first he ran towards the bridge over the river and turned his steps towards the big town. But on the bridge the unfortunate fugitive stopped. The kingly crown on his brow was quite gone. It had disappeared as if it had been spun of sunbeams. He was deeply bent with sorrow; his whole body shook; his heart throbbed; his brain burned like fire.

Then he thought he saw the Spirit of Fasting coming towards him for the third time. She was much more friendly, much more compassionate than before; but she seemed to him only so much the more terrible.

"Alas, unhappy one," she said, "surely this must be the last of your pranks! You have wished to celebrate the festival of love during that time of fasting which is called life; but you see what happens to you. Come now and be faithful to me; you have tried everything and have only me to whom to turn."

He waved his arm to keep her off. "I know what you wish of me. You wish to lead me back to work and renunciation, but I cannot. Not now, not now!"

The pallid Spirit of Fasting smiled ever more mildly. "You are innocent, Petter Nord. Do not grieve so over what you have not caused! Was not Edith kind to you? Did you not see that she had forgiven you? Come with me to your work! Live, as you have lived!"

The boy cried more vehemently. "Is it any better for me, do you think, that I have killed just her who has been kind to me, her, who cares for me? Had it not been better if I had murdered someone whom I wished to murder. I must make amends. I must save her life. I cannot think of work now."

"Oh, you madman," said the Spirit of Fasting, "the festival of reparation which you wish to celebrate is the greatest audacity of all."

Then Petter Nord rebelled absolutely against his friend of many years. He scoffed at her. "What have you made me believe?" he said. "That you were a tiresome and peevish old woman with arms full of small, harmless twigs. You are a sorceress of life. You are a monster. You are beautiful, and you are terrible. You yourself know no bounds nor limits; why should I know them? How can you preach fasting, you, who wish to deluge me with such an overmeasure of sorrow? What are the festivals I have celebrated compared to those you are continually preparing for me! Begone with your pallid moderation! Now I wish to be as mad as yourself."

Not one step could he take towards the big town. Neither could he turn directly round and again go the length of the one street in the village; he took the path up the mountain, climbed to the enchanted pine-wood, and wandered about among the stiff, prickly young trees, until a friendly path led him to the graveyard. There he found a hiding place in a corner where the pines grew high as masts, and there he threw himself weary unto death on the ground.

He almost lost consciousness. He did not know if time passed or if everything stood still. But after a while steps were heard, and he woke to a feeble consciousness. He seemed to have been far, far away. He saw a funeral procession draw near, and instantly a confused thought rose in him. How long had he lain there? Was Edith dead already? Was she looking for him here? Was the corpse in the coffin hunting for its murderer? He shook and sweated. He lay well hidden in the dark pine thicket; but he trembled for what might happen if the corpse found him. He bent aside the branches and looked out. A hunted deserter could not have spied more wildly after his pursuers.

The funeral was that of a poor man. The attendance was small. The coffin was lowered without wreaths into the grave. There was no sign of tears on any of the faces. Petter Nord had still enough sense to see that this could not be Edith Halfvorson's funeral train.

But if this was not she, who knows if it was not a greeting from her. Petter Nord felt that he had no right to escape. She had said that he was to go up to the graveyard. She must have meant that he was to wait for her there, so that she could find him to give him his punishment. The funeral was a greeting, a token. She wished him to wait for her there.

To his sick brain the low churchyard wall rose as high as a rampart. He stared despairingly at the frail trellis-gate; it was like the most solid door of oak. He was imprisoned. He could never get away, until she herself came up and brought him his punishment.

What she was going to do with him he did not know. Only one thing was distinct and clear; that he must wait here until she came for him. Perhaps she would take him with her into the grave; perhaps she would command him to throw himself from the mountain. He could not know – he must wait for a while yet.

Reason fought a despairing struggle: "You are innocent, Petter Nord. Do not grieve over what you have not caused! She has not sent you any messages. Go down to your work! Lift your foot and you are over the wall; push with one finger and the gate is open."

No, he could not. Most of the time he was in a stupor, a trance. His thoughts were indistinct, as when on the point of falling asleep. He only knew one thing, that he must stay where he was.

The news came to her lying and fading in emulation with the rootless birches. "Petter Nord, with whom you played one summer day, is in the graveyard waiting for you. Petter Nord, whom your uncle has frightened out of his senses, cannot leave the graveyard until your flower-decked coffin comes to fetch him."

The girl opened her eyes as if to look at the world once more. She sent a message to Petter Nord. She was angry at his mad pranks. Why could she not die in peace? She had never wished that he should have any pangs of conscience for her sake.

The bearer of the message came back without Petter Nord. He could not come. The wall was too high and the gate too strong. There was only one who could free him.

During those days they thought of nothing else in the little town. "He is there; he is there still," they told one another every day. "Is he mad?" they asked most often, and some who had talked with him answered that he certainly would be when "she" came. But they were exceedingly proud of that martyr to love who gave a glory to the town. The poor took him food. The rich stole up on the mountain to catch a glimpse of him.

But Edith, who could not move, who lay helpless and dying, she who had so much time to think, with what was she occupying herself? What thoughts revolved in her brain day and night? Oh, Petter Nord, Petter Nord! Must she always see before her the man who loved her, who was losing his mind for her sake, who really, actually was in the graveyard waiting for her coffin.

See, that was something for the steel-spring in her nature. That was something for her imagination, something for her benumbed senses.

To think what he meant to do when she should come! To imagine what he would do if she should not come there as a corpse!

They talked of it in the whole town, talked of it and nothing else. As the cities of ancient times had loved their martyrs, the little village loved the unhappy Petter Nord; but no one liked to go into the graveyard and talk to him. He looked wilder each day. The obscurity of madness sank ever closer about him. "Why does she not try to get well?" they said of Edith. "It is unjust of her to die."

Edith was almost angry. She who was so tired of life, must she be compelled to take up the heavy burden again? But nevertheless she began an honest effort. She felt what a work of repairing and mending was going on in her body with seething force during these weeks. And no material was spared. She consumed incredible quantities of those things which give strength and life, whatever they may be: malt extract or cod-liver oil, fresh air or sunshine, dreams or love.

And what glorious days they were, long, warm, and sunny!

At last she got the doctor's permission to be carried up there. The whole town was in alarm when she undertook the journey. Would she come down with a madman? Could the misery of those weeks be blotted out of his brain? Would the exertions she had made to begin life again be profitless? And if it were so, how would it go with her?

As she passed by, pale with excitement, but still full of hope, there was cause enough for anxiety. No one concealed from themselves that Petter Nord had taken quite too large a place in her imagination. She was the most eager of all in the worship of that strange saint. All restraints had fallen from her when she had heard what he suffered for her sake. But how would the sight of him affect her enthusiasm? There is nothing romantic in a madman.

When she had been carried up to the gate of the graveyard, she left her bearers and walked alone up the broad middle path. Her gaze wandered round the flowering spot, but she saw no one.

Suddenly she heard a faint rustle in a clump of fir trees, and she saw a wild, distorted face staring from it. Never had she seen terror so plainly stamped on a face. She was frightened herself at the sight of it, mortally frightened. She could hardly restrain herself from running away.

Then a great, holy feeling welled up in her. There was no longer any thought of love or enthusiasm, but only grief that a fellow-being, one of the unhappy ones who passed through the vale of tears with her, should be destroyed.

The girl remained. She did not give way a single step; she let him slowly accustom himself to the sight of her. But she put all the strength she possessed in her gaze. She drew the man to her with the whole force of the will that had conquered the illness in herself.

He came forward out of his corner, pale, wild and unkempt. He advanced towards her, but the terror never left his face. He looked as if he were fascinated by a wild beast, which came to tear him to pieces. When he was quite close to her, she put both her hands on his shoulders and looked smiling into his face.

"Come, Petter Nord, what is the matter with you? You must go from here! What do you mean by staying so long up here in the graveyard, Petter Nord?"

He trembled and sank down. But she felt that she subdued him with her eyes. Her words, on the other hand, seemed to have absolutely no meaning to him.

She changed her tone a little. "Listen to what I say, Petter Nord. I am not dead. I am not going to die. I have got well in order to come up here and save you."

He still stood in the same dull terror. Again there came a change in her voice. "You have not caused my death," she said more tenderly, "you have given me life."

She repeated it again and again. And her voice at last was trembling with emotion, thick with weeping. But he did not understand anything of what she said.

"Petter Nord, I love you so much, so much!" she burst out.

He was just as unmoved.

She knew nothing more to try with him. She would have to take him down with her to the town and let time and care help.

It is not easy to say what the dreams she had taken up there with her were and what she had expected from this meeting with the man who loved her. Now, when she was to give it all up and treat him as a madman only, she felt such pain, as if she was about to lose the dearest thing life had given her. And in that bitterness of loss she drew him to her and kissed him on the forehead.

It was meant as a farewell to both happiness and life. She felt her strength fail her. A mortal weakness came over her.

But then she thought she saw a feeble sign of life in him. He was not quite so limp and dull. His features were twitching. He trembled more and more violently. She watched with ever-growing alarm. He was waking, but to what? At last he began to weep.

She led him away to a tomb. She sat down on it, pulled him down in front of her and laid his bead on her lap. She sat and caressed him, while he wept.

He was like someone waking from a nightmare.

"Why am I weeping?" he asked himself. "Oh, I know; I had such a terrible dream. But it is not true. She is alive. I have not killed her. So foolish to weep for a dream."

Gradually everything grew clear to him; but his tears continued to flow. She sat and caressed him, but he wept still for a long time.

"I feel such a need of weeping," he said.

Then he looked up and smiled. "Is it Easter now?" he asked.

"What do you mean by now?"

"It can be called Easter, when the dead rise again," he continued. Thereupon, as if they had been intimate many years, he began to tell her about the Spirit of Fasting and of his revolt against her rule.

"It is Easter now, and the end of her reign," she said.

But when he realized that Edith was sitting there and caressing him, he had to weep again. He needed so much to weep. All the distrust of life which misfortunes had brought to the little Värmland boy needed tears to wash it away. Distrust that love and joy, beauty and strength blossomed on the earth, distrust in himself, all must go, all did go, for if was Easter; the dead lived and the Spirit of Fasting would never again *come into power.*

The Legend of the Bird's Nest

Hatto the hermit stood in the wilderness and prayed to God. A storm was raging, and his long beard and matted hair waved about him like weather-beaten tufts of grass on the summit of an old ruin. But he did not push his hair out of his eyes, nor did he tuck his beard into his belt, for his arms were uplifted in prayer. Ever since sunrise he had raised his gnarled, hairy arms towards heaven, as untiringly as a tree stretches up its branches, and he meant to remain standing so till night. He had a great boon to pray for.

He was a man who had suffered much of the world's anger. He had himself persecuted and tortured, and persecutions and torture from others had fallen to his share, more than his heart could bear. So he went out on the great heath, dug himself a hole in the riverbank and became a holy man, whose prayers were heard at God's throne.

Hatto the hermit stood there on the riverbank by his hole and prayed the great prayer of his life. He prayed God that He should appoint the day of doom for this wicked world. He called on the trumpet-blowing angels, who were to proclaim the end of the reign of sin. He cried out to the waves of the sea of blood, which were to drown the unrighteous. He called on the pestilence, which should fill the churchyards with heaps of dead.

Round about stretched a desert plain. But a little higher up on the riverbank stood an old willow with a short trunk, which swelled out at the top in a great knob like a head, from which new, light-green shoots grew out. Every autumn it was robbed of these strong, young branches by the inhabitants of that fuel-less heath. Every spring the tree put forth new, soft shoots, and in stormy weather these waved and fluttered about it, just as hair and beard fluttered about Hatto the hermit.

A pair of wagtails, which used to make their nest in the top of the willow's trunk among the sprouting branches, had intended to begin their building that very day. But among the whipping shoots the birds found no quiet. They came flying with straws and root fibers and dried sedges, but they had to turn back with their errand unaccomplished. Just then they noticed old Hatto, who called upon God to make the storm seven times more violent, so that the nests of the little birds might be swept away and the eagle's aerie destroyed.

Of course no one now living can conceive how mossy and dried-up and gnarled and black and unlike a human being such an old plain-dweller could be. The skin was so drawn over brow and cheeks, that he looked almost like a death's-head, and one saw only by a faint gleam in the hollows of the eye sockets that he was alive. And the dried-up muscles of the body gave it no roundness, and the upstretched, naked arms consisted only of shapeless bones, covered with shriveled, hardened, barklike skin. He wore an old, close-fitting, black robe. He was tanned by the sun and black with dirt. His hair and beard alone were light, bleached by the rain and sun, until they had become the same green-grey color as the under side of the willow leaves.

The birds, flying about, looking for a place to build, took Hatto the hermit for another old willow tree, checked in its struggle towards the sky by axe and saw like the first one. They circled about him many times, flew away and came again, took their landmarks, considered his position in regard to birds of prey and winds, found him rather unsatisfactory, but nevertheless decided in his favor, because he stood so near to the river and to the tufts of sedge, their larder and storehouse. One of them shot swift as an arrow down into his upstretched hand and laid his root fiber there.

There was a lull in the storm, so that the root-fiber was not torn instantly away from the hand; but in the hermit's prayers there was no pause: "May the Lord come soon to destroy this world of corruption, so that man may not have time to heap more sin upon himself! May he save the unborn from life! For the living there is no salvation."

Then the storm began again, and the little root-fiber fluttered away out of the hermit's big gnarled hand. But the birds came again and tried to wedge the foundation of the new home in between the fingers. Suddenly a shapeless and dirty thumb laid itself on the straws and held them fast, and four fingers arched themselves so that there was a quiet niche to build in. The hermit continued his prayers.

"Oh Lord, where are the clouds of fire which laid Sodom waste? When wilt Thou let loose the floods which lifted the ark to Ararat's top? Are not the cups of Thy patience emptied and the vials of Thy grace exhausted? Oh Lord, when wilt Thou rend the heavens and come?"

And feverish visions of the Day of Doom appeared to Hatto the hermit. The ground trembled, the heavens glowed. Across the flaming sky he saw black clouds of flying birds, a horde of panic-stricken beasts rushed, roaring and bellowing, past him. But while his soul was occupied with these fiery visions, his eyes began to follow the flight of the little birds, as they flashed to and fro and with a cheery peep of satisfaction wove a new straw into the nest.

The old man had no thought of moving. He had made a vow to pray without moving with uplifted hands all day in order to force the Lord to grant his request. The more exhausted his body became, the more vivid visions filled his brain. He heard the walls of cities fall and the houses crack. Shrieking, terrified crowds rushed by him, pursued by the angels of vengeance and destruction, mighty forms with stern, beautiful faces, wearing silver coats of mail, riding black horses and swinging scourges, woven of white lightning.

The little wagtails built and shaped busily all day, and the work progressed rapidly. On the tufted heath with its stiff sedges and by the river with its reeds and rushes, there was no lack of building material. They had no time for noon siesta nor for evening rest. Glowing with eagerness and delight, they flew to and fro, and before night came they had almost reached the roof.

But before night came, the hermit had begun to watch them more and more. He followed them on their journeys; he scolded them when they built foolishly; he was furious when the wind disturbed their work; and least of all could he endure that they should take any rest.

Then the sun set, and the birds went to their old sleeping place in among the rushes.

Let him who crosses the heath at night bend clown until his face comes on a level with the tufts of grass, and he will see a strange spectacle outline itself against the western sky. Owls with great, round wings skim over the ground, invisible to anyone standing upright. Snakes glide about there, lithe, quick, with narrow heads uplifted on swanlike necks. Great turtles crawl slowly forward, hares and water-rats flee before preying beasts, and a fox bounds after a bat, which is chasing mosquitoes by the river. It seems as if every tuft has come to life. But through it all the little birds sleep on the waving rushes, secure from all harm in that resting-place which no enemy can approach, without the water splashing or the reeds shaking and waking them.

When the morning came, the wagtails believed at first that the events of the day before had been a beautiful dream.

They had taken their landmarks and flew straight to their nest, but it was gone. They flew searching over the heath and rose up into the air to spy about. There was not a trace of nest or tree. At last they lighted on a couple of stones by the riverbank and considered. They wagged their long tails and cocked their heads on one side. Where had the tree and nest gone?

But hardly had the sun risen a hand's-breadth over the belt of trees on the other bank, before their tree came walking and placed itself on the same spot where it had been the day before. It was just as black and gnarled as ever and bore their nest on the top of something, which must be a dry, upright branch.

Then the wagtails began to build again, without troubling themselves anymore about nature's many wonders.

Hatto the hermit, who drove the little children away from his hole telling them that it had been best for them if they had never been born, he who rushed out into the mud to hurl curses after the joyous young people who rowed up the stream in pleasure-boats, he from whose angry eyes the shepherds on the heath guarded their flocks, did not return to his place by the river for the sake of the little birds. He knew that not only has every letter in the holy books its hidden, mysterious meaning, but so also has everything which God allows to take place in nature. He had thought out the meaning of the wagtails building in his hand. God wished him to remain standing with uplifted arms until the birds had raised their brood; and if he should have the power to do that, he would be heard.

But during that day he did not see so many visions of the Day of Doom. Instead, he watched the birds more and more eagerly. He saw the nest soon finished. The little builders fluttered about it and inspected it. They went after a few bits of lichen from the real willow tree and fastened them on the outside, to fill the place of plaster and paint. They brought the finest cotton-grass, and the female wagtail took feathers from her own breast and lined the nest.

The peasants, who feared the baleful power that the hermit's prayers might have at the throne of God, used to bring him bread and milk to mitigate his wrath. They came now too and found him standing motionless, with the bird's nest in his hand. "See how the holy man loves the little creatures," they said, and were no longer afraid of him, but lifted the bowl of milk to his mouth and put the bread between his lips. When he had eaten and drunk, he drove away the people with angry words, but they only smiled at his curses.

His body had long since become the slave of his will. By hunger and blows, by praying all day, by waking a week at a time, he had taught it obedience. Now the steellike muscles held his arms uplifted for days and weeks, and when the female wagtail began to sit on her eggs and never left the nest, he did not return to his hole even at night. He learned to sleep sitting, with upstretched arms. Among the dwellers in the wilderness there are many who have done greater things.

He grew accustomed to the two little, motionless bird-eyes which stared down at him over the edge of the nest. He watched for hail and rain, and sheltered the nest as well as he could.

At last one day the female is freed from her duties. Both the birds sit on the edge of the nest, wag their tails and consult and look delighted, although the whole nest seems to be full of an anxious peeping. After a while they set out on the wildest hunt for midges.

Midge after midge is caught and brought to whatever it is that is peeping up there in his hand. And when the food comes, the peeping is at its very loudest. The holy man is disturbed in his prayers by that peeping.

And gently, gently he bends his arm, which has almost lost the power of moving, and his little fiery eyes stare down into the nest.

Never had he seen anything so helplessly ugly and miserable: small, naked bodies, with a little thin down, no eyes, no power of flight, nothing really but six big, gaping mouths.

It seemed very strange to him, but he liked them just as they were. Their father and mother he had never spared in the general destruction, but when hereafter he called to God to ask of Him the salvation of the world through its annihilation, he made a silent exception of those six helpless ones.

When the peasant women now brought him food, he no longer thanked them by wishing their destruction. Since he was necessary to the little creatures up there, he was glad that they did not let him starve to death.

Soon six round heads were to be seen the whole day long stretching over the edge of the nest. Old Hatto's arm sank more and more often to the level of his eyes. He saw the feathers push out through the red skin, the eyes open, the bodies round out. Happy inheritors of the beauty nature has given to flying creatures, they developed quickly in their loveliness.

And during all this time prayers for the great destruction rose more and more hesitatingly to old Hatto's lips. He thought that he had God's promise, that it should come when the little birds were fledged. Now he seemed to be searching for a loophole for God the Father. For these six little creatures, whom he had sheltered and cherished, he could not sacrifice.

It was another matter before, when he had not had anything that was his own. The love for the small and weak, which it has been every little child's mission to teach big, dangerous people, came over him and made him doubtful.

He sometimes wanted to hurl the whole nest into the river, for he thought that they who die without sorrow or sin are the happy ones. Should he not save them from beasts of prey and cold, from hunger, and from life's manifold visitations? But just as he thought this, a sparrow-hawk came swooping down on the nest. Then Hatto seized the marauder with his left hand, swung him about his head and hurled him with the strength of wrath out into the stream.

The day came at last when the little birds were ready to fly. One of the wagtails was working inside the nest to push the young ones out to the edge, while the other flew about, showing them how easy it was, if they only dared to try. And when the young ones were obstinate and afraid, both the parents flew about, showing them all their most beautiful feats of flight. Beating with their wings, they flew in swooping curves, or rose right up like larks or hung motionless in the air with vibrating wings.

But as the young ones still persist in their obstinacy, Hatto the hermit cannot keep from mixing himself up in the matter. He gives them a cautious shove with his finger and then it is done. Out they go, fluttering and uncertain, beating the air like bats, sink, but rise again, grasp what the art is and make use of it to reach the nest again as quickly as possible. Proud and rejoicing, the parents come to them again and old Hatto smiles.

It was he who gave the final touch after all.

He now considered seriously if there could not be any way out of it for our Lord.

Perhaps, when all was said, God the Father held this earth in His right hand like a big bird's nest, and perhaps He had come to cherish love for all those who build and dwell there, for all earth's defenseless children. Perhaps He felt pity for those whom He had promised to destroy, just as the hermit felt pity for the little birds.

Of course the hermit's birds were much better than our Lord's people, but he could quite understand that God the Father nevertheless had love for them.

The next day the bird's nest stood empty, and the bitterness of loneliness filled the heart of the hermit. Slowly his arm sank down to his side, and it seemed to him as if all nature held its breath to listen for the thunder of the trumpet of Doom. But just then all the wagtails came again and lighted on his head and shoulders, for they were not at all afraid of him. Then a ray of light shot through old Hatto's confused brain. He had lowered his arm, lowered it every day to look at the birds.

And standing there with all the six young ones fluttering and playing about him, he nodded contentedly to someone whom he did not see. "I let you off," he said, "I let you off. I have not kept my word, so you need not keep yours."

And it seemed to him as if the mountains ceased to tremble and as if the river laid itself down in easy calm in its bed.

The King's Grave

It was at the time of year when the heather is red. It grew over the sand-hills in thick clumps. From low treelike stems close-growing green branches raised their hardy ever-green leaves and unfading flowers. They seemed not to be made of ordinary, juicy flower substance, but of dry, hard scales. They were very insignificant in size and shape; nor was their fragrance of much account. Children of the open moors, they had not unfolded in the still air where lilies open their alabaster petals; nor did they grow in the rich soil from which roses draw nourishment for their swelling crowns. What made them flowers was really their color, for they were glowing red. They had received the color-giving sunshine in plenty. They were no pallid cellar growth; the blessed gaiety and strength of health lay over all the blossoming heath.

The heather covered the bare fields with its red mantle up to the edge of the wood. There, on a gently sloping ridge, stood some ancient, half ruined stone cairns; and however closely the heather tried to creep to these, there were always rents in its web, through which were visible great, flat rocks, folds in the mountain's own rough skin. Under the biggest of these piles rested an old king, Atle by name. Under the others slumbered those of his warriors who had fallen when the great battle raged on the moor. They had lain there now so long that the fear and respect of death had departed from their graves. The path ran between their resting-places. The wanderer by night never thought to look whether forms wrapped in mist sat at midnight on the tops of the cairns staring in silent longing at the stars.

It was a glittering morning, dewy and warm. The hunter who had been out since daybreak had thrown himself down in the heather behind King Atle's pile. He lay on his back and slept. He had dragged his hat down over his eyes; and under his head lay his leather game-bag, out of which protruded a hare's long ears and the bent tail-feathers of a black-cock. His bow and arrows lay beside him.

From out of the wood came a girl with a bundle in her hand. When she reached the flat rock between the piles of stones, she thought what a good place it would be to dance. She was seized with an ardent desire to try. She laid her bundle on the heather and began to dance quite alone. She had no idea that a man lay asleep behind the king's cairn.

The hunter still slept. The heather showed burning red against the deep blue of the sky. An anthill stood close beside the sleeper. On it lay a piece of quartz, which sparkled as if it had wished to set fire to all the old stubble of the heath. Above the hunter's head the black-cock feathers spread out like a plume, and their iridescence shifted from deep purple to steely blue. On the unshaded part of his face the burning sunshine glowed. But he did not open his eyes to look at the glory of the morning.

In the meanwhile the girl continued to dance, and whirled about so eagerly that the blackened moss which had collected in the unevennesses of the rocks flew about her. An old, dry fir root, smooth and grey with age, lay upturned among the heather. She took it and whirled about with it. Chips flew out from the moldering wood. Centipedes and earwigs that had lived in the crevices scurried out head over heels into the luminous air and bored down among the roots of the heather.

When the swinging skirts grazed the heather, clouds of small grey butterflies fluttered up from it. The under side of their wings was white and silvery and they whirled like dry leaves in a squall. They then seemed quite white, and it was as if a red sea threw up white foam. The butterflies remained for a short time in the air. Their fragile wings fluttered so violently that the down loosened and fell like thin silver white feathers. The air seemed to be filled with a glorified mist.

On the heath grasshoppers sat and scraped their back legs against their wings, so that they sounded like harp strings. They kept good time and played so well together, that to anyone passing over the moor it sounded like the same grasshopper during the whole walk, although it seemed to be first on the right, then on the left; now in front, now behind. But the dancer was not content with their playing and began after a little while to hum the measure of a dance tune. Her voice was shrill and harsh. The hunter was waked by the song. He turned on his side, raised himself to his elbow, and looked over the pile of stones at the dancing girl.

He had dreamt that the hare which he had just killed had leaped out of the bag and had taken his own arrows to shoot at him. He now stared at the girl half awake, dizzy with his dream, his head burning from sleeping in the sun.

She was tall and coarsely built, not fair of face, nor light in the dance, nor tuneful in her song. She had broad cheeks, thick lips and a flat nose.

She had very red cheeks, very dark hair. She was exuberant in figure, moving with vigor and life. Her clothes were shabby but bright in color. Red bands edged the striped skirt and bright colored worsted fringes outlined the seams of her bodice. Other young maidens resemble roses and lilies, but she was like the heather, strong, gay and glowing.

The hunter watched with pleasure as the big, splendid woman danced on the red heath among the playing grasshoppers and the fluttering butterflies. While he looked at her he laughed so that his mouth was drawn up towards his ears. But then she suddenly caught sight of him and stood motionless.

"I suppose you think I am mad," was the first thing that occurred to her to say. At the same time she wondered how she would get him to hold his tongue about what he had seen. She did not care to hear it told down in the village that she had danced with a fir root.

He was a man poor in words. Not a syllable could he utter. He was so shy that he could think of nothing better than to run away, although he longed to stay. Hastily he got his hat on his head and his leather bag on his back. Then he ran away through the clumps of heather.

She snatched up her bundle and ran after him. He was small, stiff in his movements and evidently had very little strength. She soon caught up with him and knocked his hat off to induce him to stop. He really wished to do so, but he was confused with shyness and fled with still greater speed. She ran after him and began to pull at his game-bag. Then he had to stop to defend it. She fell upon him with all her strength. They fought, and she threw him to the ground. "Now he will not speak of it to anyone," she thought, and rejoiced.

At the same moment, however, she grew sick with fright, for the man who lay on the ground turned livid and his eyes rolled inwards in his head. He was not hurt in any way, however. He could not bear emotion. Never before had so strong and conflicting feelings stirred within that lonely forest dweller. He rejoiced over the girl and was angry and ashamed and yet proud that she was so strong. He was quite out of his head with it all.

The big, strong girl put her arm under his back and lifted him up. She broke the heather and whipped his face with the stiff twigs until the blood came back to it. When his little eyes again turned towards the light of day, they shone with pleasure at the sight of her. He was still silent; but he drew forward the hand which she had placed about his waist and caressed it gently.

He was a child of starvation and early toil. He was dry and pallid, thin and anemic. She was touched by his faintheartedness; he who nevertheless seemed to be about thirty years old. She thought that he must live quite alone in the forest since he was so pitiful and so meanly dressed. He could have no one to look after him, neither mother nor sister nor sweetheart.

The great compassionate forest spread over the wilderness. Concealing and protecting, it took to its heart everything which sought its help. With its lofty trunks it kept watch by the lair of the fox and the bear, and in the twilight of the thick bushes it hid the egg-filled nests of little birds.

At the time when people still had slaves, many of them escaped to the woods and found shelter behind its green walls. It became a great prison for them which they did not dare to leave. The forest held its prisoners in strict discipline. It forced the dull ones to use their wits and educated those ruined by slavery to order and honor. Only to the industrious did it give the right to live.

The two who met on the heath were descendants of such prisoners of the forest. They sometimes went down to the inhabited, cultivated valleys, for they no longer feared to be reduced to the slavery from which their forefathers had fled, but they were happiest in the dimness of the forest. The hunter's name was Tönne. His real work was to cultivate the earth, but he also could do other things. He collected herbs, boiled tar, dried punk, and often went hunting. The dancer was called Jofrid. Her father was a charcoal burner. She tied brooms, picked juniper berries and brewed ale of the white-flowering myrtle. They were both very poor.

They had never met before in the big wood, but now they thought that all its paths wound into a net, in which they ran forward and back and could not possibly escape one another. They never knew how to choose a way where they did not meet.

Tönne had once had a great sorrow. He had lived with his mother for a long while in a miserable, wattled but, but as soon as he was grown up he was seized with the idea to build her a warm cabin. During all his leisure moments he went into the clearing, cut down trees and hewed them into squared pieces. Then he hid the timber in dark crannies under moss and branches. It was his intention that his mother should not know anything of all this work before he was ready to build the house. But his mother died before he could show her what he had collected; before he had time to tell her what he had wished to do. He, who had worked with the same zeal as David, King of Israel, when he gathered treasures for the temple of God, grieved most bitterly over it. He lost all interest in the building. For him the brushwood shelter was good enough. Yet he was hardly better off in his home than an animal in its hole.

When he, who had always heretofore crept about alone, was now seized with the desire to seek Jofrid's company, it certainly meant that he would like to have her for his sweetheart and his bride. Jofrid also waited daily for him to speak to her father or to herself about the matter. But Tönne could not. This showed that he was of a race of slaves. The thoughts that came into his head moved as slowly as the sun when he travels across the sky. And it was more difficult for him to shape those thoughts to connected speech than for a smith to forge a bracelet out of rolling grains of sand.

One day Tönne took Jofrid to one of the clefts, where he had hidden his timber. He pulled aside the branches and moss and showed her the squared beams. "That was to have been mother's house," he said. The young girl was strangely slow in understanding a young man's thoughts. When he showed her his mother's logs she ought to have understood, but she did not understand.

Then he decided to make his meaning even plainer. A few days later he began to drag the logs up to the place between the cairns, where he had seen Jofrid for the first time. She came as usual along the path and saw him at work. Nevertheless she went on without saying anything. Since they had become friends she had often given him a good handshake, but she did not seem to want to help him with the heavy work. Tönne still thought that she ought to have understood that it was now her house which he meant to build.

She understood it very well, but she had no desire to give herself to such a man as Tönne. She wished to have a strong and healthy husband. She thought it would be a poor livelihood to marry anyone who was weak and dull. Still, there was much which drew her to that silent, shy man. She thought how hard he had worked to gladden his mother and had not enjoyed the happiness of being ready in time. She could weep for his sake. And now he was building the house just where he had seen her dance. He had a good heart. And that interested her and fixed her thoughts on him, but she did not at all wish to marry him.

Every day she went over the heather field and saw the log cabin grow, miserable and without windows, with the sunlight filtering in through the leaky walls.

Tönne's work progressed very quickly, but not with care. His timbers were not bent square, the lark was scarcely taken off. He laid the floor with split young trees. It was uneven and shaky. The heather, which grew and blossomed under it, – for at year had passed since the day when Tönne had lain aleep behind King Atle's pile, – pushed up bold red clusters through the cracks, and ants without number wandered out and in, inspecting the fragile work of man.

Wherever Jofrid went during those days, the thought never left her that a house was being built for her there. A home was being prepared for her upon the heath. And she knew that if she did not enter there as mistress, the bear and the fox would make it their home. For she knew Tönne well enough to understand that if he found he had worked in vain, he would never move into the new house. He would weep, poor man, when he heard that she would not live there. It would be a new sorrow for him, as deep as when his mother died. But he had himself to blame, because he had not asked her in time.

She thought that she gave him a sufficient hint in not helping him with the house. She often felt impelled to do so. Every time she saw any soft, white moss, she wanted to pick it to fill in the leaky walls. She longed, too, to help Tönne to build the chimney. As he was making it, all the smoke would gather in the house. But it did not matter how it was. No food would ever be cooked there, no ale brewed. Still it was odious that the house would never leave her thoughts.

Tönne worked, glowing with eagerness, certain that Jofrid would understand his meaning, if only the house were ready. He did not wonder much about her; he had enough to do to hew and shape. The days went quickly for him.

One afternoon, when Jofrid came over the moor, she saw that there was a door in the cottage and a slab of stone for a threshold. Then she understood that everything must now be ready, and she was much agitated. Tönne had covered the roof with tufts of flowering heather, and she was seized by an intense longing to enter under that red roof. He was not at the new house and she decided to go in. The house was built for her. It was her home. It was not possible to resist the desire to see it.

Within it was more attractive than she had expected. Rushes were strewed over the floor. It was full of the fresh fragrance of pine and resin. The sunshine that played through the windows and cracks made bands of light through the air. It looked as if she had been expected; in the crannies of the wall green branches were stuck, and in the fireplace stood a newly cut fir tree. Tönne had not moved in his old furniture. There was nothing but a new table and a bench, over which an elk skin was thrown.

As soon as Jofrid had crossed the threshold, she felt the pleasant coziness of home surrounding her. She was happy and content while she stood there, but to leave it seemed to her as hard as to go away and serve strangers. It happened that Jofrid had expended much hard work in procuring a kind of dower for herself. With skillful hands she had woven bright colored fabrics, such as are used to adorn a room, and she wanted to put them up in her own home, when she got one. Now she wondered how those cloths would look here. She wished she could try them in the new house.

She hurried quickly home, fetched her roll of weavings and began to fasten the bright-colored pieces of cloth up under the roof. She threw open the door to let the big setting sun shine on her and her work. She moved eagerly about the cottage, brisk, gay, bumming a merry tune. She was perfectly happy. It looked so fine. The woven roses and stars shone as never before.

While she worked she kept a good look-out over the moor and the graves, for it seemed to her as if Tönne might now too be lying hidden behind one of the cairns and laughing at her. The king's grave lay opposite the door and behind it she saw the sun setting. Time after time she looked out. She felt as if someone was sitting there and watching her.

Just as the sun was so low that only a few blood-red beams filtered over the old stone heap, she saw who it was who was watching her. The whole pile of stones was no longer stones, but a mighty, old warrior, who was sitting there, scarred and grey, and staring at her. Round about his head the rays of the sun made a crown, and his red mantle was so wide that it spread over the whole moor. His head was big and heavy, his face grey as stone. His clothes and weapons were also stone-colored, and repeated so exactly the shadings and mossiness of the rock, that one had to look closely to see that it was a warrior and not a pile of stones. It was like those insects which resemble tree-twigs. One can go by them twenty times before one sees that it is a soft animal body one has taken for hard wood.

But Jofrid could no longer be mistaken. It was the old King Atle himself sitting there. She stood in the doorway, shaded her eyes with her hand, and looked right into his stony face. He had very small, oblique eyes under a domelike brow, a broad nose and a long beard. And he was alive, that man of stone. He smiled and winked at her. She was afraid, and what terrified her most of all were his thick, muscular arms and hairy hands. The longer she looked at him the broader grew his smile, and at last he lifted one of his mighty arms to beckon her to him. Then Jofrid took flight towards home.

But when Tönne came home and saw the house adorned with starry weavings, he found courage to send a friend to Jofrid's father. The latter asked Jofrid what she thought about it and she gave her consent. She was well pleased with the way it had turned out, even if she had been half forced to give her hand. She could not say no to the man, to whose house she had already carried her dower. Still she looked first to see that old King Atle had again become a pile of stones.

Tönne and Jofrid lived happily for many years. They earned a good reputation. "They are good," people said. "See how they stand by one another, see how they work together, see how one cannot live apart from the other!"

Tönne grew stronger, more enduring and less heavy-witted every day. Jofrid seemed to have made a whole man of him. Almost always he let her rule, but he also understood how to carry out his own will with tenacious obstinacy.

Jests and merriment followed Jofrid wherever she went. Her clothes became more vivid the older she grew. Her whole face was bright red. But in Tönne's eyes she was beautiful.

They were not so poor as many others of their class. They ate butter with their porridge and mixed neither bran nor bark in their bread. Myrtle ale foamed in their tankards. Their flocks of sheep and goats increased so quickly that they could allow themselves meat.

Tönne once worked for a peasant in the valley. The latter, who saw how he and his wife worked together with great gaiety, thought like many another: "See, these are good people."

The peasant had lately lost his wife, and she had left behind her a child six months old. He asked Tönne and Jofrid to take his son as a foster-child.

"The child is very dear to me," he said, "therefore I give it to you, for you are good people."

They had no children of their own, so that it seemed very fitting for them to take it. They accepted it too without hesitation. They thought it would be to their advantage to bring up a peasant's child, besides which they expected to be cheered in their old age by their foster-son.

But the child did not live to grow up with them. Before the year was out it was dead. It was said by many that it was the fault of the foster-parents, for the child had been unusually strong before it came to them. By that no one meant, however, that they had killed it intentionally, but rather that they had undertaken something beyond their powers. They had not had sense or love enough to give it the care it needed. They were accustomed only to think of themselves and to look out for themselves. They had no time to care for a child. They wished to go together to their work every day and to sleep a quiet sleep at night. They thought that the child drank too much of their good milk and did not allow him as much as themselves. They had no idea that they were treating the boy badly. They thought that they were just as tender to him as parents generally are. It seemed more to them as if their foster-son had been a punishment and a torment. They did not mourn him when he died.

Women usually enjoy nothing better than to take care of a child; but Jofrid had a husband, whom she often had to care for like a mother, so that she desired no one else. They also love to see their children's quick growth; but Jofrid had pleasure enough in watching Tönne develop sense and manliness, in adorning and taking care of her house, in the increase of their flocks, and in the crops which they were raising below on the moor.

Jofrid went to the peasant's farm and told him that the child was dead. Then the man said: "I am like the man who puts cushions in his bed so soft that he sinks down to the hard bottom. I wished to care too well for my son, and look, now he is dead!" And he was heart-broken.

At his words Jofrid began to weep bitterly. "Would to God that you had not left your son with us!" she said. "We were too poor. He could not get what he needed with us."

"That is not what I meant," answered the peasant. "I believe that you have overindulged the child. But I will not accuse anyone, for over life and death God alone rules. Now I mean to celebrate the funeral of my only son with the same expense as if he had been full grown, and to the feast I invite both Tönne and you. By that you may know that I bear you no grudge."

So Tönne and Jofrid went to the funeral banquet. They were well treated, and no one said anything unfriendly to them. The women who had dressed the child's body had related that it had been miserably thin and had borne marks of great neglect. But that could easily come from sickness. No one wished to believe anything bad about the foster-parents, for it was known that they were good people.

Jofrid wept a great deal during those days, especially when she heard the women tell how they had to wake and toil for their little children. She noticed, too, that the women at the funeral were continually talking of their children. Some rejoiced so in them that they never could stop telling of their questions and games. Jofrid would have liked to have talked about Tönne, but most of them never spoke of their husbands.

Late one evening Jofrid and Tönne came home from the festivities. They went straight to bed. But hardly had they fallen asleep before they were waked by a feeble crying. "It is the child," they thought, still half asleep, and were angry at being disturbed. But suddenly both of them sat right up in the bed. The child was dead. Where did that crying come from? When they were quite awake, they heard nothing, but as soon as they began to drop off to sleep they heard it. Little, tottering feet sounded on the stone threshold outside the house, a little hand groped for the door, and when it could not open it, the child crept crying and feeling along the wall, until it stopped just outside where they were sleeping. As soon as they spoke or sat up, they perceived nothing; but when they tried to sleep, they distinctly heard the uncertain steps and the suppressed sobbings.

That which they had not wished to believe, but which seemed a possibility during these last days, now became a certainty. They felt that they had killed the child. Why otherwise should it have the power to haunt them?

From that night all happiness left them. They lived in constant fear of the ghost. By day they had some peace, but at night they were so disturbed by the child's weeping and choking sobs, that they did not dare to sleep alone. Jofrid often went long distances to get someone to stop over night in their house. If there was any stranger there, it was quiet, but as soon as they were alone, they heard the child.

One night, when they had found no one to keep them company and could not sleep for the child, Jofrid got up from her bed.

"You sleep, Tönne," she said. "If I keep awake, we will not hear anything."

She went out and sat down on the doorstep, thinking of what they ought to do to get peace, for they could not go on living as things were. She wondered if confession and penance and mortification and repentance could relieve them from this heavy punishment.

Then it happened that she raised her eyes and saw the same vision as once before from this place. The pile of stones had changed to a warrior. The night was quite dark, but still she could plainly see that old King Atle sat there and watched her. She saw him so well that she could distinguish the moss-grown bracelets on his wrists and could see how his legs were bound with crossed bands, between which his calf muscles swelled.

This time she was not afraid of the old man. He seemed to be a friend and consoler in her unhappiness. He looked at her with pity, as if he wished to give her courage. Then she thought that the mighty warrior had once had his day, when he had overthrown hundreds of enemies there on the heath and waded through the streams of blood that had poured between the clumps. What had he thought of one dead man more or less? How much would the sight of children, whose fathers he had killed, have moved his heart of stone? Light as air would the burden of a child's death have rested on his conscience.

And she heard his whisper, the same which the old stone-cold heathenism had whispered through all time. "Why repent? The gods rule us. The fates spin the threads of life. Why shall the children of earth mourn because they have done what the immortal gods have forced them to do?"

Then Jofrid took courage and said to herself: "How am I to blame because the child died? It is God alone who decides. Nothing takes place without his will." And she thought that she could lay the ghost by putting all repentance from her.

But now the door opened and Tönne came out to her. "Jofrid," he said, "it is in the house now. It came up and knocked on the edge of the bed and woke me. What shall we do, Jofrid?"

"The child is dead," said Jofrid. "You know that it is lying deep underground. All this is only dreams and imagination." She spoke hardly and coldly, for she feared that Tönne would do something reckless, and thereby cause them misfortune.

"We must put an end to it," said Tönne.

Jofrid laughed dismally. "What do you wish to do? God has sent this to us. Could He not have kept the child alive if He had chosen? He did not wish it, and now He persecutes us for its death. Tell me by what right He persecutes us?"

She got her words from the old stone warrior, who sat dark and high on his pile. It seemed as if he suggested to her everything she answered Tönne.

"We must acknowledge that we have neglected the child, and do penance," said Tönne.

"Never will I suffer for what is not my fault," said Jofrid. "Who wanted the child to die? Not I, not I. What kind of a penance will you do? You need all your strength for work."

"I have already tried with scourging," said Tönne. "It is of no avail."

"You see," she said, and laughed again.

"We must try something else," Tönne went on with persistent determination. "We must confess."

"What do you want to tell God, that He does not know?" mocked Jofrid. "Does He not guide your thoughts, Tönne? What will you tell Him?" She thought that Tönne was stupid and obstinate. She had found him so in the beginning of their acquaintance, but since then she had not thought of it, but had loved him for his good heart.

"We will confess to the father, Jofrid, and offer him compensation."

"What will you offer him?" she asked.

"The house and the goats."

"He will certainly demand an enormous compensation for his only son. All that we possess would not be enough."

"We will give ourselves as slaves into his power, if he is not content with less."

At these words Jofrid was seized by cold despair, and she hated Tönne from the depths of her soul. Everything she would lose appeared so plainly to her, – freedom, for which her ancestors had ventured their lives, the house, her comforts, honor and happiness.

"Mark my words, Tönne," she said hoarsely, half choked with pain, "that the day you do that thing will be the day of my death."

After that no more words were exchanged between them, but they remained sitting on the doorstep until the day came. Neither found a word to appease or to conciliate; each felt fear and scorn of the other. The one measured the other by the standard of his own anger, and they found each other narrow-minded and bad-tempered.

After that night Jofrid could not refrain from letting Tönne feel that he was her inferior. She let him understand in the presence of others that he was stupid, and helped him with his work so that he had to think how much stronger she was. She evidently wished to take away from him all rights as master of the house. Sometimes she pretended to be very lively, to distract him and to prevent him from brooding. He had not done anything to carry out his plan, but she did not believe that he had given it up.

During this time Tönne became more and more as he was before his marriage. He grew thin and pale, silent and slow-witted. Jofrid's despair increased each day, for it seemed as if everything was to be taken from her. Her love for Tönne came back, however, when she saw him unhappy. "What is any of it worth to me if Tönne is ruined?" she thought. "It is better to go into slavery with him than to see him die in freedom."

Jofrid, however, could not at once decide to obey Tönne. She fought a long and severe fight. But one morning she awoke in an unusually calm and gentle mood. Then she thought that she could now do what he demanded. And she waked him, saying that it should be as he wished. Only that one day he should grant her to say farewell to everything.

The whole forenoon she went about strangely gentle. Tears rose easily to her eyes. The heath was beautiful that day for her sake, she thought. Frost had passed over it, the flowers were gone, and the whole moor had turned brown. But when it was lighted by the slanting rays of the autumn sun, it looked as if the heather glowed red once more. And she remembered the day when she saw Tönne for the first time.

She wished that she might see the old king once more, for he had helped her to find her happiness. She had been seriously afraid of him of late. She felt as if he were lying in wait to seize her. But now she thought he could no longer have any power over her. She would remember to look for him towards night when the moon rose.

It happened that a couple of wandering musicians came by about noon. Jofrid had the idea to ask them to stop at her house the whole afternoon, for she wished to have a dance. Tönne had to hasten to her parents and ask them to come. And her small brothers and sisters ran down to the village for the other guests. Soon many people had collected.

There was great gaiety. Tönne kept apart in a corner of the house, as was his habit when they had guests, but Jofrid was quite wild in her fun. With shrill voice she led the dance and was eager in offering her guests the foaming ale. There was not much room in the cottage, but the fiddlers were untiring, and the dance went on with life and spirit. It grew suffocatingly warm. The door was thrown open, and all at once Jofrid saw that night had come and that the moon had risen. Then she went to the door and looked out into the white world of the moonlight.

A heavy dew had fallen. The whole heath was white, as the moon was reflected in all the little drops, which had collected on every twig. There Tönne and she would go tomorrow hand in hand to meet the most terrible dishonor. For, however the meeting with the peasant should turn out, whatever he might take or whatever he might let them keep, dishonor would certainly be their lot. They, who that evening possessed a good cottage and many friends, tomorrow would be despised and detested by all, perhaps they would also be robbed of everything they had earned, perhaps, too, be dishonored slaves. She said to herself: "It is the way of death." And now she could not understand how she would ever have the strength to walk in it. It seemed to her as if she were of stone, a heavy stone image like old King Atle. Although she was alive, she felt as if she would not be able to lift her heavy stone limbs to walk that way.

She turned her eyes towards the king's grave and distinctly saw the old warrior sitting there. But now he was adorned as for a feast. He no longer wore the grey, moss-grown stone attire, but white, glittering silver. Now again he wore a crown of beams, as when she first saw him, but this one was white. And white shone his breastplate and armlets, shining white were sword, hilt, and shield. He sat and watched her with silent indifference. The unfathomable mystery which great stone faces wear had now sunk down over him. There he sat dark and mighty, and Jofrid had a faint, indistinct idea that he was an image of something which was in herself and in all men, of something which was buried in faraway centuries, covered by many stones, and still not dead. She saw him, the old king, sitting deep in the human heart. Over its barren field he spread his wide king's mantle. There pleasure danced, there love of display flaunted. He was the great stone warrior who saw famine and poverty pass by without his stone heart being moved. "It is the will of the gods," he said. He was the strong man of stone, who could bear unatoned-for sin without yielding. He always said: "Why grieve for what you have done, compelled by the immortal gods?"

Jofrid's breast was shaken by a sigh deep as a sob. She had a feeling which she could not explain, a feeling that she ought to struggle with the man of stone, if she was to be happy. But at the same time she felt helplessly weak.

Her impenitence and the struggle out on the heath seemed to her to be one and the same thing, and if she could not conquer the first by some means or other, the last would gain power over her.

She looked back towards the cottage, where the weavings glowed under the roof timbers, where the musicians spread merriment, and where everything she loved was, then she felt that she could not go into slavery. Not even for Tönne's sake could she do it. She saw his pale face within in the house, and she asked herself with a contraction of the heart if he was worth the sacrifice of everything for his sake.

In the cottage the people had started a new dance. They arranged themselves in a long line, took each other by the hand, and with a wild, strong young man at the head, they rushed forward at dizzy speed. The leader drew them through the open door out cm to the moonlit heath. They stormed by Jofrid, panting and wild, stumbling against stones, falling into the heather, making wide rings round the house, circling about the heaps of stones. The last of the line called to Jofrid and stretched out his hand to her. She seized it and ran too.

It was not a dance, only a mad rush; but there was pleasure in it, audacity and the joy of living. The rings became bolder, the cries sounded louder, the laughter more boisterous. From cairn to cairn, as they lay scattered over the heath, wound the line of dancers. If anyone fell in the wild swinging, he was dragged up, the slow ones were driven onward; the musicians stood in the doorway and played the faster. There was no time to rest, to think, nor to look about. The dance went on at always madder speed over the yielding moss and slippery rocks.

During all this Jofrid felt more and more clearly that she wished to keep her freedom, that she would rather die than lose it. She saw that she could not follow Tönne. She thought of running away, of hurrying into the wood and never coming back.

They had circled about all the cairns except that of King Atle. Jofrid saw that they were now turning towards it and she kept her eyes fixed on the stone man. Then she saw how his giant arms were stretched towards the rushing dancers. She screamed aloud, but she was answered by loud laughter. She wished to stop, but a strong grasp drew her on. She saw him snatch at those hurrying by, but they were so quick that the heavy arms could not reach any of them. It was incomprehensible to her that no one saw him. The agony of death came over her. She thought that he would reach her. It was for her that he had lain in wait for many years. With the others it was only play. It was she whom he would seize at last.

Her turn came to rush by King Atle. She saw how he raised himself and bent for a spring to be sure of the matter and catch her. In her extreme need she felt that if she only could decide to give in the next day, he would not have the power to catch her, but she could not. – She came last, and she was swung so violently that she was more dragged and jerked forward than running herself, and it was hard for her to keep from falling. And although she passed at lightning speed, the old warrior was too quick for her. The heavy arms sank down over her, the stone hands seized her, she was drawn into the silvery harness of that breast. The agony of death took more and more hold of her, but she knew to the very last that it was because she had not been able to conquer the stone king in her own heart that Atle had power over her.

It was the end of the dancing and merriment. Jofrid lay dying. In the violence of their mad rout, she had been thrown against the king's cairn and received her death-blow on its stones.

The Outlaws

A peasant who had murdered a monk took to the woods and was made an outlaw. He found there before him in the wilderness another outlaw, a fisherman from the outermost islands, who had been accused of stealing a herring net. They joined together, lived in a cave, set snares, sharpened darts, baked bread on a granite rock and guarded one another's lives. The peasant never left the woods, but the fisherman, who had not committed such an abominable crime, sometimes loaded game on his shoulders and stole down among men. There he got in exchange for black-cocks, for long-eared hares and fine-limbed red deer, milk and butter, arrow-heads and clothes. These helped the outlaws to sustain life.

The cave where they lived was dug in the side of a hill. Broad stones and thorny sloe-bushes hid the entrance. Above it stood a thick growing pine tree. At its roots was the vent-hole of the cave. The rising smoke filtered through the tree's thick branches and vanished into space. The men used to go to and from their dwelling-place, wading in the mountain stream, which ran down the hill. No-one looked for their tracks under the merry, bubbling water.

At first they were hunted like wild beasts. The peasants gathered as if for a chase of bear or wolf. The wood was surrounded by men with bows and arrows. Men with spears went through it and left no dark crevice, no bushy thicket unexplored. While the noisy battue hunted through the wood, the outlaws lay in their dark hole, listening breathlessly, panting with terror. The fisherman held out a whole day, but he who had murdered was driven by unbearable fear out into the open, where he could see his enemy. He was seen and hunted, but it seemed to him seven times better than to lie still in helpless inactivity. He fled from his pursuers, slid down precipices, sprang over streams, climbed up perpendicular mountain walls. All latent strength and dexterity in him was called forth by the excitement of danger. His body became elastic like a steel spring, his foot made no false step, his hand never lost its hold, eye and ear were twice as sharp as usual. He understood what the leaves whispered and the rocks warned. When he had climbed up a precipice, he turned towards his pursuers, sending them gibes in biting rhyme. When the whistling darts whizzed by him, he caught them, swift as lightning, and hurled them down on his enemies. As he forced his way through whipping branches, something within him sang a song of triumph.

The bald mountain ridge ran through the wood and alone on its summit stood a lofty fir. The red-brown trunk was bare, but in the branching top rocked an eagle's nest. The fugitive was now so audaciously bold that he climbed up there, while his pursuers looked for him on the wooded slopes. There he sat twisting the young eaglets' necks, while the hunt passed by far below him. The male and female eagle, longing for revenge, swooped down on the ravisher. They fluttered before his face, they struck with their beaks at his eyes, they beat him with their wings and tore with their claws bleeding weals in his weather beaten skin. Laughing, he fought with them. Standing upright in the shaking nest, he cut at them with his sharp knife and forgot in the pleasure of the play his danger and his pursuers. When he found time to look for them, they had gone by to some other part of the forest. No one had thought to look for their prey on the bald mountain-ridge. No one had raised his eyes to the clouds to see him practicing boyish tricks and sleep-walking feats while his life was in the greatest danger.

The man trembled when he found that he was paved. With shaking hands he caught at a support, giddy he measured the height to which he had climbed. And moaning with the fear of falling, afraid of the birds, afraid of being seen, afraid of everything, he slid down the trunk. He laid himself down on the ground, so as not to be seen, and dragged himself forward over the rocks until the underbrush covered him. There he hid himself under the young pine tree's tangled branches. Weak and powerless, he sank down on the moss. A single man could have captured him.

Tord was the fisherman's name. He was not more than sixteen years old, but strong and bold. He had already lived a year in the woods.

The peasant's name was Berg, with the surname Rese. He was the tallest and the strongest man in the whole district, and moreover handsome and well-built. He was broad in the shoulders and slender in the waist. His hands were as well shaped as if he had never done any hard work. His hair was brown and his skin fair. After he had been some time in the woods he acquired in all ways a more formidable appearance. His eyes became piercing, his eyebrows grew bushy, and the muscles which knitted them lay finger thick above his nose. It showed now more plainly than before how the upper part of his athlete's brow projected over the lower. His lips closed more firmly than of old, his whole face was thinner, the hollows at the temples grew very deep, and his powerful jaw was much more prominent. His body was less well filled out but his muscles were as hard as steel. His hair grew suddenly grey.

Young Tord could never weary of looking at this man. He had never before seen anything so beautiful and powerful. In his imagination he stood high as the forest, strong as the sea. He served him as a master and worshipped him as a god. It was a matter of course that Tord should carry the hunting spears, drag home the game, fetch the water and build the fire. Berg Rese accepted all his services, but almost never gave him a friendly word. He despised him because he was a thief.

The outlaws did not lead a robber's or brigand's life; they supported themselves by hunting and fishing. If Berg Rese had not murdered a holy man, the peasants would soon have ceased to pursue him and have left him in peace in the mountains. But they feared great disaster to the district, because he who had raised his hand against the servant of God was still unpunished. When Tord came down to the valley with game, they offered him riches and pardon for his own crime if he would show them the way to Berg Rese's hole, so that they might take him while he slept. But the boy always refused; and if anyone tried to sneak after him up to the wood, he led him so cleverly astray that he gave up the pursuit.

Once Berg asked him if the peasants had not tried to tempt him to betray him, and when he heard what they had offered him as a reward, he said scornfully that Tord had been foolish not to accept such a proposal.

Then Tord looked at him with a glance, the like of which Berg Rese had never before seen. Never had any beautiful woman in his youth, never had his wife or child looked so at him. "You are my lord, my elected master," said the glance. "Know that you may strike me and abuse me as you will, I am faithful notwithstanding."

After that Berg Rese paid more attention to the boy and noticed that he was bold to act but timid to speak. He had no fear of death. When the ponds were first frozen, or when the bogs were most dangerous in the spring, when the quagmires were hidden under richly flowering grasses and cloudberry, he took his way over them by choice. He seemed to feel the need of exposing himself to danger as a compensation for the storms and terrors of the ocean, which he had no longer to meet. At night he was afraid in the woods, and even in the middle of the day the darkest thickets or the wide-stretching roots of a fallen pine could frighten him. But when Berg Rese asked him about it, he was too shy to even answer.

Tord did not sleep near the fire, far in in the cave, on the bed which was made soft with moss and warm with skins, but every night, when Berg had fallen asleep, he crept out to the entrance and lay there on a rock. Berg discovered this, and although he well understood the reason, he asked what it meant. Tord would not explain. To escape anymore questions, he did not lie at the door for two nights, but then he returned to his post.

One night, when the drifting snow whirled about the forest tops and drove into the thickest underbrush, the driving snowflakes found their way into the outlaws' cave. Tord, who lay just inside the entrance, was, when he waked in the morning, covered by a melting snowdrift. A few days later he fell ill. His lungs wheezed, and when they were expanded to take in air, he felt excruciating pain. He kept up as long as his strength held out, but when one evening he leaned down to blow the fire, he fell over and remained lying.

Berg Rese came to him and told him to go to his bed. Tord moaned with pain and could not raise himself. Berg then thrust his arms under him and carried him there. But he felt as if he had got hold of a slimy snake; he had a taste in the mouth as if he had eaten the unholy horseflesh, it was so odious to him to touch the miserable thief.

He laid his own big bearskin over him and gave him water, more he could not do. Nor was it anything dangerous. Tord was soon well again. But through Berg's being obliged to do his tasks and to be his servant, they had come nearer to one another. Tord dared to talk to him when he sat in the cave in the evening and cut arrow shafts.

"You are of a good race, Berg," said Tord. "Your kinsmen are the richest in the valley. Your ancestors have served with kings and fought in their castles."

"They have oftener fought with bands of rebels and done the kings great injury," replied Berg Rese.

"Your ancestors gave great feasts at Christmas, and so did you, when you were at home. Hundreds of men and women could find a place to sit in your big house, which was already built before Saint Olof first gave the baptism here in Viken. You owned old silver vessels and great drinking-horns, which passed from man to man, filled with mead."

Again Berg Rese had to look at the boy. He sat up with his legs hanging out of the bed and his head resting on his hands, with which he at the same time held back the wild masses of hair which would fall over his eyes. His face had become pale and delicate from the ravages of sickness. In his eyes fever still burned. He smiled at the pictures he conjured up: at the adorned house, at the silver vessels, at the guests in gala array and at Berg Rese, sitting in the seat of honor in the hall of his ancestors. The peasant thought that no one had ever looked at him with such shining, admiring eyes, or thought him so magnificent, arrayed in his festival clothes, as that boy thought him in the torn skin dress.

He was both touched and provoked. That miserable thief had no right to admire him.

"Were there no feasts in your house?" he asked.

Tord laughed. "Out there on the rocks with father and mother! Father is a wrecker and mother is a witch. No one will come to us."

"Is your mother a witch?"

"She is," answered Tord, quite untroubled. "In stormy weather she rides out on a seal to meet the ships over which the waves are washing, and those who are carried overboard are hers."

"What does she do with them?" asked Berg.

"Oh, a witch always needs corpses. She makes ointments out of them, or perhaps she eats them. On moonlight nights she sits in the surf, where it is whitest, and the spray dashes over her. They say that she sits and searches for shipwrecked children's fingers and eyes."

"That is awful," said Berg.

The boy answered with infinite assurance: "That would be awful in others, but not in witches. They have to do so."

Berg Rese found that he had here come upon a new way of regarding the world and things.

"Do thieves have to steal, as witches have to use witchcraft?" he asked sharply.

"Yes, of course," answered the boy; "everyone has to do what he is destined to do." But then he added, with a cautious smile: "There are thieves also who have never stolen."

"Say out what you mean," said Berg.

The boy continued with his mysterious smile, proud at being an unsolvable riddle: "It is like speaking of birds who do not fly, to talk of thieves who do not steal."

Berg Rese pretended to be stupid in order to find out what he wanted. "No one can be called a thief without having stolen," he said.

"No; but," said the boy, and pressed his lips together as if to keep in the words, "but if someone had a father who stole," he hinted after a while.

"One inherits money and lands," replied Berg Rese, "but no one bears the name of thief if he has not himself earned it."

Tord laughed quietly. "But if somebody has a mother who begs and prays him to take his father's crime on him. But if such a one cheats the hangman and escapes to the woods. But if someone is made an outlaw for a fish-net which he has never seen."

Berg Rese struck the stone table with his clenched fist. He was angry. This fair young man had thrown away his whole life. He could never win love, nor riches, nor esteem after that. The wretched striving for food and clothes was all which was left him. And the fool had let him, Berg Rese, go on despising one who was innocent. He rebuked him with stern words, but Tord was not even as afraid as a sick child is of its mother, when she chides it because it has caught cold by wading in the spring brooks.

On one of the broad, wooded mountains lay a dark tarn. It was square, with as straight shores and as sharp corners as if it had been cut by the hand of man. On three sides it was surrounded by steep cliffs, on which pines clung with roots as thick as a man's arm. Down by the pool, where the earth had been gradually washed away, their roots stood up out of the water, bare and crooked and wonderfully twisted about one another. It was like an infinite number of serpents which had wanted all at the same time to crawl up out of the pool but had got entangled in one another and been held fast. Or it was like a mass of blackened skeletons of drowned giants which the pool wanted to throw up on the land. Arms and legs writhed about one another, the long fingers dug deep into the very cliff to get a hold, the mighty ribs formed arches, which held up primeval trees. It had happened, however, that the iron arms, the steellike fingers with which the pines held themselves fast, had given way, and a pine had been borne by a mighty north wind from the top of the cliff down into the pool. It had burrowed deep down into the muddy bottom with its top and now stood there. The smaller fish had a good place of refuge among its branches, but the roots stuck up above the water like a many-armed monster and contributed to make the pool awful and terrifying.

On the tarn's fourth side the cliff sank down. There a little foaming stream carried away its waters. Before this stream could find the only possible way, it had tried to get out between stones and tufts, and had by so doing made a little world of islands, some no bigger than a little hillock, others covered with trees.

Here where the encircling cliffs did not shut out all the sun, leafy trees flourished. Here stood thirsty, grey-green alders and smooth-leaved willows. The birch tree grew there as it does everywhere where it is trying to crowd out the pine woods, and the wild cherry and the mountain ash, those two which edge the forest pastures, filling them with fragrance and adorning them with beauty. Here at the outlet there was a forest of reeds as high as a man, which made the sunlight fall green on the water just as it falls on the moss in the real forest. Among the reeds there were open places; small, round pools, and water-lilies were floating there. The tall stalks looked down with mild seriousness on those sensitive beauties, who discontentedly shut their white petals and yellow stamens in a hard, leatherlike sheath as soon as the sun ceased to show itself.

One sunshiny day the outlaws came to this tarn to fish. They waded out to a couple of big stones in the midst of the reed forest and sat there and threw out bait for the big, green-striped pickerel that lay and slept near the surface of the water.

These men, who were always wandering in the woods and the mountains, had, without their knowing it themselves, come under nature's rule as much as the plants and the animals. When the sun shone, they were open-hearted and brave, but in the evening, as soon as the sun had disappeared, they became silent; and the night, which seemed to them much greater and more powerful than the day, made them anxious and helpless. Now the green light, which slanted in between the rushes and colored the water with brown and dark-green streaked with gold, affected their mood until they were ready for any miracle. Every outlook was shut off. Sometimes the reeds rocked in an imperceptible wind, their stalks rustled, and the long, ribbonlike leaves fluttered against their faces. They sat in grey skins on the grey stones. The shadows in the skins repeated the shadows of the weather-beaten, mossy stone. Each saw his companion in his silence and immovability change into a stone image. But in among the rushes swam mighty fishes with rainbow-colored backs. When the men threw out their hooks and saw the circles spreading among the reeds, it seemed as if the motion grew stronger and stronger, until they perceived that it was not caused only by their cast. A sea-nymph, half human, half a shining fish, lay and slept on the surface of the water. She lay on her back with her whole body under water. The waves so nearly covered her that they had not noticed her before. It was her breathing that caused the motion of the waves. But there was nothing strange in her lying there, and when the next instant she was gone, they were not sure that she had not been only an illusion.

The green light entered through the eyes into the brain like a gentle intoxication. The men sat and stared with dulled thoughts, seeing visions among the reeds, of which they did not dare to tell one another. Their catch was poor. The day was devoted to dreams and apparitions.

The stroke of oars was heard among the rushes, and they started up as from sleep. The next moment a flat-bottomed boat appeared, heavy, hollowed out with no skill and with oars as small as sticks. A young girl, who had been picking water-lilies, rowed it. She had dark-brown hair, gathered in great braids, and big dark eyes; otherwise she was strangely pale. But her paleness toned to pink and not to grey. Her cheeks had no higher color than the rest of her face, the lips had hardly enough. She wore a white linen shirt and a leather belt with a gold buckle. Her skirt was blue with a red hem. She rowed by the outlaws without seeing them. They kept breathlessly still, but not for fear of being seen, but only to be able to really see her. As soon as she had gone they were as if changed from stone images to living beings. Smiling, they looked at one another.

"She was white like the water-lilies," said one. "Her eyes were as dark as the water there under the pine-roots."

They were so excited that they wanted to laugh, really laugh as no one had ever laughed by that pool, till the cliffs thundered with echoes and the roots of the pines loosened with fright.

"Did you think she was pretty?" asked Berg Rese.

"Oh, I do not know, I saw her for such a short time. Perhaps she was."

"I do not believe you dared to look at her. You thought that it was a mermaid."

And they were again shaken by the same extravagant merriment.

Tord had once as a child seen a drowned man. He had found the body on the shore on a summer day and had not been at all afraid, but at night he had dreamed terrible dreams. He saw a sea, where every wave rolled a dead man to his feet. He saw, too, that all the islands were covered with drowned men, who were dead and belonged to the sea, but who still could speak and move and threaten him with withered white hands.

It was so with him now. The girl whom he had seen among the rushes came back in his dreams. He met her out in the open pool, where the sunlight fell even greener than among the rushes, and he had time to see that she was beautiful. He dreamed that he had crept up on the big pine root in the middle of the dark tarn, but the pine swayed and rocked so that sometimes he was quite under water. Then she came forward on the little islands. She stood under the red mountain ashes and laughed at him. In the last dream-vision he had come so far that she kissed him. It was already morning, and he heard that Berg Rese had got up, but he obstinately shut his eyes to be able to go on with his dream. When he awoke, he was as though dizzy and stunned by what had happened to him in the night. He thought much more now of the girl than he had done the day before.

Towards night he happened to ask Berg Rese if he knew her name.

Berg looked at him inquiringly. “Perhaps it is best for you to hear it,” he said. “She is Unn. We are cousins.”

Tord then knew that it was for that pale girl’s sake Berg Rese wandered an outlaw in forest and mountain. Tord tried to remember what he knew of her. Unn was the daughter of a rich peasant. Her mother was dead, so that she managed her father’s house. This she liked, for she was fond of her own way and she had no wish to be married.

Unn and Berg Rese were the children of brothers, and it had long been said that Berg preferred to sit with Unn and her maids and jest with them than to work on his own lands. When the great Christmas feast was celebrated at his house, his wife had invited a monk from Draksmark, for she wanted him to remonstrate with Berg, because he was forgetting her for another woman. This monk was hateful to Berg and to many on account of his appearance. He was very fat and quite white. The ring of hair about his bald head, the eyebrows above his watery eyes, his face, his hands and his whole cloak, everything was white. Many found it hard to endure his looks.

At the banquet table, in the hearing of all the guests, this monk now said, for he was fearless and thought that his words would have more effect if they were heard by many, "People are in the habit of saying that the cuckoo is the worst of birds because he does not rear his young in his own nest, but here sits a man who does not provide for his home and his children, but seeks his pleasure with a strange woman. Him will I call the worst of men." – Unn then rose up. "That, Berg, is said to you and me," she said. "Never have I been so insulted, and my father is not here either." She had wished to go, but Berg sprang after her. "Do not move!" she said. "I will never see you again." He caught up with her in the hall and asked her what he should do to make her stay. She had answered with flashing eyes that he must know that best himself. Then Berg went in and killed the monk.

Berg and Tord were busy with the same thoughts, for after a while Berg said: "You should have seen her, Unn, when the white monk fell. The mistress of the house gathered the small children about her and cursed her. She turned their faces towards her, that they might forever remember her who had made their father a murderer. But Unn stood calm and so beautiful that the men trembled. She thanked me for the deed and told me to fly to the woods. She bade me not to be robber, and not to use the knife until I could do it for an equally just cause."

"Your deed had been to her honor," said Tord.

Berg Rese noticed again what had astonished him before in the boy. He was like a heathen, worse than a heathen; he never condemned what was wrong. He felt no responsibility. That which must be, was. He knew of God and Christ and the saints, but only by name, as one knows the gods of foreign lands. The ghosts of the rocks were his gods. His mother, wise in witchcraft, had taught him to believe in the spirits of the dead.

Then Berg Rese undertook a task which was as foolish as to twist a rope about his own neck. He set before those ignorant eyes the great God, the Lord of justice, the Avenger of misdeeds, who casts the wicked into places of everlasting torment. And he taught him to love Christ and his mother and the holy men and women, who with lifted hands kneeled before God's throne to avert the wrath of the great Avenger from the hosts of sinners. He taught him all that men do to appease God's wrath. He showed him the crowds of pilgrims making pilgrimages to holy places, the flight of self-torturing penitents and monks from a worldly life.

As he spoke, the boy became more eager and more pale, his eyes grew large as if for terrible visions. Berg Rese wished to stop, but thoughts streamed to him, and he went on speaking. The night sank down over them, the black forest night, when the owls hoot. God came so near to them that they saw his throne darken the stars, and the chastising angels sank down to the tops of the trees. And under them the fires of Hell flamed up to the earth's crust, eagerly licking that shaking place of refuge for the sorrowing races of men.

The autumn had come with a heavy storm. Tord went alone in the woods to see after the snares and traps. Berg Rese sat at home to mend his clothes. Tord's way led in a broad path up a wooded height.

Every gust carried the dry leaves in a rustling whirl up the path. Time after time Tord thought that someone went behind him. He often looked round. Sometimes he stopped to listen, but he understood that it was the leaves and the wind, and went on. As soon as he started on again, he heard someone come dancing on silken foot up the slope. Small feet came tripping. Elves and fairies played behind him. When he turned round, there was no one, always no one. He shook his fists at the rustling leaves and went on.

They did not grow silent for that, but they took another tone. They began to hiss and to pant be hind him. A big viper came gliding. Its tongue dripping venom hung far out of its mouth, and its bright body shone against the withered leaves. Beside the snake pattered a wolf, a big, gaunt monster, who was ready to seize fast in his throat when the snake had twisted about his feet and bitten him in the heel. Sometimes they were both silent, as if to approach him unperceived, but they soon betrayed themselves by hissing and panting, and sometimes the wolf's claws rung against a stone. Involuntarily Tord walked quicker and quicker, but the creatures hastened after him. When he felt that they were only two steps distant and were preparing to strike, he turned. There was nothing there, and he had known it the whole time.

He sat down on a stone to rest. Then the dry leaves played about his feet as if to amuse him. All the leaves of the forest were there: small, light yellow birch leaves, red speckled mountain ash, the elm's dry, dark-brown leaves, the aspen's tough light red, and the willow's yellow green. Transformed and withered, scarred and torn were they, and much unlike the downy, light green, delicately shaped leaves, which a few months ago had rolled out of their buds.

"Sinners," said the boy, "sinners, nothing is pure in God's eyes. The flame of his wrath has already reached you."

When he resumed his wandering, he saw the forest under him bend before the storm like a heaving sea, but in the path it was calm. But he heard what he did not feel. The woods were full of voices.

He heard whisperings, wailing songs, coarse threats, thundering oaths. There was laughter and laments, there was the noise of many people. That which hounded and pursued, which rustled and hissed, which seemed to be something and still was nothing, gave him wild thoughts. He felt again the anguish of death, as when he lay on the floor in his den and the peasants hunted him through the wood. He heard again the crashing of branches, the people's heavy tread, the ring of weapons, the resounding cries, the wild, bloodthirsty noise, which followed the crowd.

But it was not only that which he heard in the storm. There was something else, something still more terrible, voices which he could not interpret, a confusion of voices, which seemed to him to speak in foreign tongues. He had heard mightier storms than this whistle through the rigging, but never before had he heard the wind play on such a many-voiced harp. Each tree had its own voice; the pine did not murmur like the aspen nor the poplar like the mountain ash. Every hole had its note, every cliff's sounding echo its own ring. And the noise of the brooks and the cry of foxes mingled with the marvelous forest storm. But all that he could interpret; there were other strange sounds. It was those which made him begin to scream and scoff and groan in emulation with the storm.

He had always been afraid when he was alone in the darkness of the forest. He liked the open sea and the bare rocks. Spirits and phantoms crept about among the trees.

Suddenly he heard who it was who spoke in the storm. It was God, the great Avenger, the God of justice. He was hunting him for the sake of his comrade. He demanded that he should deliver up the murderer to His vengeance.

Then Tord began to speak in the midst of the storm. He told God what he had wished to do, but had not been able. He had wished to speak to Berg Rese and to beg him to make his peace with God, but he had been too shy. Bashfulness had made him dumb. "When I heard that the earth was ruled by a just God," he cried, "I understood that he was a lost man. I have lain and wept for my friend many long nights. I knew that God would find him out, wherever he might hide. But I could not speak, nor teach him to understand. I was speechless, because I loved him so much. Ask not that I shall speak to him, ask not that the sea shall rise up against the mountain."

He was silent, and in the storm the deep voice, which had been the voice of God for him, ceased. It was suddenly calm, with a sharp sun and a splashing as of oars and a gentle rustle as of stiff rushes. These sounds brought Unn's image before him. – The outlaw cannot have anything, not riches, nor women, nor the esteem of men. – If he should betray Berg, he would be taken under the protection of the law. – But Unn must love Berg, after what he had done for her. There was no way out of it all.

When the storm increased, he heard again steps behind him and sometimes a breathless panting. Now he did not dare to look back, for he knew that the white monk went behind him. He came from the feast at Berg Rese's house, drenched with blood, with a gaping axe-wound in his forehead. And he whispered: "Denounce him, betray him, save his soul. Leave his body to the pyre, that his soul may be spared. Leave him to the slow torture of the rack, that his soul may have time to repent."

Tord ran. All this fright of what was nothing in itself grew, when it so continually played on the soul, to an unspeakable terror. He wished to escape from it all. As he began to run, again thundered that deep, terrible voice, which was God's. God himself hunted him with alarms, that he should give up the murderer. Berg Rese's crime seemed more detestable than ever to him. . An unarmed man had been murdered, a man of God pierced with shining steel. It was like a defiance of the Lord of the world. And the murderer dared to live! He rejoiced in the sun's light and in the fruits of the earth as if the Almighty's arm were too short to reach him.

He stopped, clenched his fists and howled out a threat. Then he ran like a madman from the wood down to the valley.

Tord hardly needed to tell his errand; instantly ten peasants were ready to follow him. It was decided that Tord should go alone up to the cave, so that Berg's suspicions should not be aroused. But where he went he should scatter peas, so that the peasants could find the way.

When Tord came to the cave, the outlaw sat on the stone bench and sewed. The fire gave hardly any light, and the work seemed to go badly. The boy's heart swelled with pity. The splendid Berg Rese seemed to him poor and unhappy. And the only thing he possessed, his life, should be taken from him. Tord began to weep.

"What is it?" asked Berg. "Are you ill? Have you been frightened?"

Then for the first time Tord spoke of his fear. "It was terrible in the wood. I heard ghosts and raw specters. I saw white monks."

"'Sdeath, boy!"

"They crowded round me all the way up Broad mountain. I ran, but they followed after and sang. Can I never be rid of the sound? What have I to do with them? I think that they could go to one who needed it more."

"Are you mad tonight, Tord?"

Tord talked, hardly knowing what words he used. He was free from all shyness. The words streamed from his lips.

"They are all white monks, white, pale as death. They all have blood on their cloaks. They drag their hoods down over their brows, but still the wound shines from under; the big, red, gaping wound from the blow of the axe."

"The big, red, gaping wound from the blow of the axe?"

"Is it I who perhaps have struck it? Why shall I see it?"

"The saints only know, Tord," said Berg Rese, pale and with terrible earnestness, "what it means that you see a wound from an axe. I killed the monk with a couple of knife-thrusts."

Tord stood trembling before Berg and wrung his hands. "They demand you of me! They want to force me to betray you!"

"Who? The monks?"

"They, yes, the monks. They show me visions. They show me her, Unn. They show me the shining, sunny sea. They show me the fishermen's camping-ground, where there is dancing and merrymaking. I close my eyes, but still I see. 'Leave me in peace,' I say. 'My friend has murdered, but he is not bad. Let me be, and I will talk to him, so that he repents and atones. He shall confess his sin and go to Christ's grave. We will both go together to the places which are so holy that all sin is taken away from him who draws near them.'"

"What do the monks answer?" asked Berg. "They want to have me saved. They want to have me on the rack and wheel."

"Shall I betray my dearest friend, I ask them," continued Tord. "He is my world. He has saved me from the bear that had his paw on my throat. We have been cold together and suffered every want together. He has spread his bear-skin over me when I was sick. I have carried wood and water for him; I have watched over him while he slept; I have fooled his enemies. Why do they think that I am one who will betray a friend? My friend will soon of his own accord go to the priest and confess, then we will go together to the land of atonement."

Berg listened earnestly, his eyes sharply searching Tord's face. "You shall go to the priest and tell him the truth," he said. "You need to be among people."

"Does that help me if I go alone? For your sin, Death and all his specters follow me. Do you not see how I shudder at you? You have lifted your hand against God himself. No crime is like yours. I think that I must rejoice when I see you on rack and wheel. It is well for him who can receive his punishment in this world and escapes the wrath to come. Why did you tell me of the just God? You compel me to betray you. Save me from that sin. Go to the priest." And he fell on his knees before Berg.

The murderer laid his hand on his head and looked at him. He was measuring his sin against his friend's anguish, and it grew big and terrible before his soul. He saw himself at variance with the Will which rules the world. Repentance entered his heart.

"Woe to me that I have done what I have done," he said. "That which awaits me is too hard to meet voluntarily. If I give myself up to the priests, they will torture me for hours; they will roast me with slow fires. And is not this life of misery, which we lead in fear and want, penance enough? Have I not lost lands and home? Do I not live parted from friends and everything which makes a man's happiness? What more is required?"

When he spoke so, Tord sprang up wild with terror. "Can you repent?" he cried. "Can my words move your heart? Then come instantly! How could I believe that! Let us escape! There is still time."

Berg Rese sprang up, he too. "You have done it, then –"

"Yes, yes, yes! I have betrayed you! But come quickly! Come, as you can repent! They will let us go. We shall escape them!"

The murderer bent down to the floor, where the battle-axe of his ancestors lay at his feet. "You son of a thief!" he said, hissing out the words, "I have trusted you and loved you."

But when Tord saw him bend for the axe, he knew that it was now a question of his own life. He snatched his own axe from his belt and struck at Berg before he had time to raise himself. The edge cut through the whistling air and sank in the bent head. Berg Rese fell head foremost to the floor, his body rolled after. Blood and brains spouted out, the axe fell from the wound. In the matted hair Tord saw a big, red, gaping hole from the blow of an axe.

The peasants came rushing in. They rejoiced and praised the deed.

"You will win by this," they said to Tord.

Tord looked down at his hands as if he saw there the fetters with which he had been dragged forward to kill him he loved. They were forged from nothing. Of the rushes' green light, of the play of the shadows, of the song of the storm, of the rustling of the leaves, of dreams were they created. And he said aloud: "God is great."

But again the old thought came to him. He fell on his knees beside the body and put his arm under him head.

"Do him no harm," he said. "He repents; he is going to the Holy Sepulcher. He is not dead, he is but a prisoner. We were just ready to go when he fell. The white monk did not want him to repent, but God, the God of justice, loves repentance."

He lay beside the body, talked to it, wept and begged the dead man to awake. The peasants arranged a bier. They wished to carry the peasant's body down to his house. They had respect for the dead and spoke softly in his presence. When they lifted him up on the bier, Tord rose, shook the hair back from his face, and said with a voice which shook with sobs, –

"Say to Unn, who made Berg Rese a murderer, that he was killed by Tord the fisherman, whose father is a wrecker and whose mother is a witch, because he taught him that the foundation of the world is justice."

The Legend of Reor

There was a man called Reor. He was from Fuglekarr in the parish of Svarteborg, and was considered the best shot in the county. He was baptized when King Olof rooted out the old belief, and was ever afterwards an eager Christian. He was freeborn, but poor; handsome, but not tall; strong, but gentle. He tamed young horses with but a look and a word, and could lure birds to him with a call. He dwelt mostly in the woods, and nature had great power over him. The growing of the plants and the budding of the trees, the play of the hares in the forest's open places and the fish's leap in the calm lake at evening, the conflict of the seasons and the changes of the weather, these were the chief events in his life. Sorrow and joy he found in such things and not in that which happened among men.

One day the skillful hunter met deep in the thickest forest an old bear and killed him with a single shot. The great arrow's sharp point pierced the mighty heart, and he fell dead at the hunter's feet. It was summer, and the bear's pelt was neither close nor even, still the archer drew it off, rolled it together into a hard bundle, and went on with the bear-skin on his back.

He had not wandered far before he perceived an extraordinarily strong smell of honey. It came from the little flowering plants that covered the ground. They grew on slender stalks, had light-green, shiny leaves, which were beautifully veined, and at the top a little spike, thickly set with white flowers. Their petals were of the tiniest, but from among them pushed up a little brush of stamens, whose pollen-filled heads trembled on white filaments. Reor thought, as he went among them, that those flowers, which stood alone and unnoticed in the darkness of the forest, were sending out message after message, summons upon summons. The strong, sweet fragrance of the honey was their cry; it spread the knowledge of their existence far away among the trees and high up towards the clouds. But there was something melancholy in the heavy perfume. The flowers had filled their cups and spread their table in expectation of their winged guests, but none came. They pined to death in the deep loneliness of the dark, windless forest thicket. They seemed to wish to cry and lament that the beautiful butterflies did not come and visit them. Where the flowers grew thickest, he thought that they sang together a monotonous song. "Come, fair guests, come today, for tomorrow we are dead, tomorrow we lie dead on the dried leaves."

Reor was permitted to see the joyous close of the flower adventure. He felt behind him a flutter as of the lightest wind and saw a white butterfly flitting about in the dimness between the thick trunks. He flew hither and thither in an uneasy quest, as if uncertain of the way. Nor was he alone; butterfly after butterfly glimmered in the darkness, until at last there was a host of white-winged honey seekers. But the first was the leader, and he found the flowers, guided by their fragrance. After him the whole butterfly host came storming. It threw itself down among the longing flowers, as the conqueror throws himself on his booty. Like a snowfall of white wings it sank down over them. And there was feasting and drinking on every flower cluster. The woods were full of silent rejoicing.

Reor went on, but now the honey-sweet fragrance seemed to follow him wherever he went. And he felt that in the wood was hidden a longing, stronger than that of the flowers, that something there drew him to itself, just as the flowers lured the butterflies. He went forward with a quiet joy in his heart, as if he was expecting a great, unknown happiness. His only fear was lest he should not be able to find the way to that which longed for him.

In front of him, on the narrow path, crawled a white snake. He bent down to pick up the luck-bringing animal, but the snake glided out of his hands and up the path. There it coiled itself and lay still; but when the huntsman again tried to catch it, glided slippery as ice between his fingers.

Reor now grew eager to possess the wisest of beasts. He ran after the snake, but was not able to reach it, and the latter lured him away from the path into the trackless forest.

It was overgrown with pines, and in such places one seldom finds grassy ground. But now the dry moss and brown pine-needles suddenly disappeared, the stiff cranberry bushes vanished, and Reor felt under foot velvet like turf. Over the green carpet trembled flower clusters, light as down, on bending stems, and between the long, narrow leaves could he seen the half-opened blossoms of the red gillyflower. It was only a little spot, and over it spread the gnarled, red-brown branches of the lofty pines, with bunches of close-growing needles. Through these the sun's rays could find many paths to the ground, and there was suffocating heat.

In the midst of the little meadow a cliff rose perpendicularly out of the ground. It lay in sharp sunshine, and the mossy stones were plainly visible, and in the fresh fractures, where the winter's frost had last loosened some mighty blocks, the long stalks of ferns clung with their brown roots in the earth-filled cracks, and on the inch-wide projections a grass-green moss lifted on needlelike stems the little, grey caps, which concealed its spores.

The cliff seemed in all ways like every other cliff, but Reor noticed instantly that he had come upon the gable-wall of a giant's house, and he discovered under moss and lichen the great hinges on which the mountain's granite door swung.

He now believed that the snake had crept in, in the grass to hide there, until it could come in among the rocks unnoticed, and he gave up all hope of catching it. He perceived now again the honey-sweet fragrance of the longing flowers and noticed that here under the cliff the heat was suffocating. It was also marvelously quiet; not a bird moved, not a leaf played in the wind; it was as if everything held its breath, waiting and listening in unspeakable tension. It was as if he had come into a room where he was not alone, although he saw no one. He thought that someone was watching him, he felt as if he had been expected. He knew no alarm, but was thrilled by a pleasant shiver, as if he were soon to see something above-the-common beautiful.

In that moment he again became aware of the snake. It had not hidden itself, it had instead crawled up on one of the blocks which the frost had broken from the cliff. And just below the white snake he saw the bright body of a girl, who lay asleep in the soft grass. She lay without any other covering than a light, weblike veil, just as if she had thrown herself down there after having taken part the whole night in some elfin dance; but the long blades of grass and the trembling flower-clusters stood high over the sleeper, so that Reor could scarcely catch a glimpse of the soft lines of her body. Nor did he go nearer in order to see better. He drew his good knife from its sheath and threw it between the girl and the cliff, so that the steel-shy daughter of the giants should not be able to flee into the mountain when she awoke.

Then he stood still in deep thought. One thing he knew, that he wished to possess the maiden who lay there; but as yet he had not quite made up his mind how he would behave towards her.

He, who knew the language of nature better than that of man, listened to the great, solemn forest and the stern mountain. "See," they said, "to you, who love the wilderness, we give our fair daughter. She will suit you better than the daughters of the plain. Reor, are you worthy of this most precious of gifts?"

Then he thanked in his heart the great, kind Nature and decided to make the maiden his wife and not merely a slave. He thought that since she had come to Christendom and human ways, she would be confused at the thought that she had lain so uncovered, so he loosened the bearskin from his back, unfolded the stiff hide, and threw the old bear's shaggy, grizzled pelt over her.

And as he did so a laugh, which made the ground shake, thundered behind the cliff. It did not sound like derision, but as if someone had sat in great fear and could not help laughing, when suddenly relieved of it. The terrible silence and oppressive heat were also at an end. Over the grass floated a cooling wind, and the pine-branches began their murmuring song. The happy huntsman felt that the whole forest had held its breath, wondering how the daughter of the wilderness would be treated by the son of man.

The snake now glided down into the high grass; but the sleeper lay bound in a magic sleep and did not move. Then Reor wrapped her in the coarse bear-skin, so that only her head showed above the shaggy fur. Although she certainly was a daughter of the old giant of the mountain, she was slender and delicately made, and the strong hunter lifted her on his arm and carried her away through the forest.

After a while he felt that someone lifted his broad-brimmed hat. He looked up and found that the giant's daughter was awake. She sat quiet on his arm, but she wished to see what the man looked like who was carrying her. He let her do as she pleased. He went on with longer strides, but said nothing.

Then she must have noticed how hot the sun burned on his head, since she had taken off his hat. She held it out over his head like a parasol, but she did not put it back, rather held it so, that she could still look down into his face. Then it seemed to him that he did not need to ask or to speak. He carried her silently down to his mother's hut. But his whole being was filled with happiness, and when he stood on the threshold of his home, he saw the white snake, which gives good fortune, glide in under its foundation.

Valdemar Atterdag

The spring that Hellqvist's great picture "Valdemar Atterdag levies a Contribution on Visby" was exhibited at the Art League, I went in there one quiet morning not knowing that that work of art was there. The big, richly colored canvas with its many figures made at the first glance an extraordinary impression. I could not look at any other picture, but went straight to that one, took a chair and sank into silent contemplation. For half an hour I lived in the Middle Ages.

Soon I was within the scene that was passing in the Visby marketplace. I saw the beer vats which began to be filled with the golden brew that King Valdemar had ordered, and the groups which gathered around them. I saw the rich merchant with his page bending under his gold and silver dishes; the young burgher who shakes his fist at the king; the monk with the sharp face who closely watches His Majesty; the ragged beggar who offers his copper; the woman who has sunk down beside one of the vats; the king on his throne; the soldiers who some swarming out of the narrow streets; the high gables, and the scattered groups of insolent guards and refractory people.

But suddenly I noticed that the chief figure of the picture is not the king, nor any of the burghers, but one of the king's steel-clad shield-bearers, the one with the closed visor.

Into that figure the artist has put a strange force. There is not a hair of him to be seen; he is steel and iron, the whole man, and yet he gives the impression of being the rightful master of the situation.

"I am Violence; I am Rapacity," he says. "It is I who am levying contribution on Visby. I am not a human being; I am merely steel and iron. My pleasure is in suffering and evil. Let them go on and torture one another. Today it is I who am lord of Visby."

"Look," he says to the beholder, "can you see that it is I who am master? As far as your eye can reach, there is nothing here but people who are torturing one another. Groaning the conquered come and leave their gold. They hate and threaten, but they obey. And the desires of the victors grow wilder the more gold they can extort. What are Denmark's king and his soldiers but my servants, at least for this one day? Tomorrow they will go to church, or sit in peaceful mirth in their inns, or also perhaps be good fathers in their own homes, but today they serve me; today they are evil-doers and ravishers."

The longer one listens to him, the better one understands what the picture is; nothing but an illustration of the old story of how people can torture one another. There is not one redeeming feature, only cruel violence and defiant hate and hopeless suffering.

Those three beer vats were to be filled that Visby should not be plundered and burned. Why do they not come, those Hanseaters, with glowing enthusiasm? Why do the women not hasten with their jewels; the revelers with their cups, the priest with his relics, eager, burning with enthusiasm for the sacrifice? "For thee, for thee, our beloved town! It is needless to send soldiers for us when it concerns thee! Oh, Visby, our mother, our honor! Take back what thou hast given us!"

But the painter has not wished to see them so, and it was not so either. No enthusiasm, only constraint, only suppressed defiance, only bewailings. Gold is everything to them, women and men sigh over that gold which they have to give.

"Look at them!" says the power that stands on the steps of the throne. "It goes to their very hearts to offer it. May he who will feel sympathy for them! They are mean, avaricious, arrogant. They are no better than the covetous brigand whom I have sent against them."

A woman has sunk down on the ground by the vats. Does it cost her so much pain to give her gold? Or is she perhaps the guilty one? Is she the cause of the laments? Is it she who has betrayed the town? Yes, it is she who has been King Valdemar's mistress. It is Ung-Hanse's daughter.

She knows well that she need give no gold. Her father's house will not be plundered, but she has collected what she possesses and brings it. In the marketplace she has been overcome by all the misery she has seen and has sunk down in infinite despair.

He had been active and merry, the young goldsmith's apprentice who served the year before in her father's house. It had been glorious to stroll at his side through this same marketplace, when the moon rose from behind the gables and illumined the beauties of Visby. She had been proud of him, proud of her father, proud of her town. And now she is lying there, broken with grief. Innocent and yet guilty! He who is sitting cold and cruel on the throne and who has brought all this devastation on the town, is he the same as the one who whispered sweet words to her? Was it to meet him that she crept, when the night before she stole her father's keys and opened the town-gate? And when she found her goldsmith's apprentice a knight with sword in hand and a steel clad host behind him, what did she think? Did she go mad at the sight of that stream of steel surging in through the gate which she had opened? Too late to bemoan, maiden! Why did you love the enemy of your town? Visby is fallen, its glory shall pass away. Why did you not throw yourself down before the gate and let the steel-shod heels trample you to death? Did you wish to live in order to see heaven's thunder-bolts strike the transgressor?

Oh maiden, at his side stands Violence and protects him. He has violated holier things than a trusting maiden. He does not even spare God's own temple. He breaks away the shining carbuncles from the church walls to fill the last vat.

The bearing of all the figures in the picture changes. Blind terror fills everything living. The wildest soldier grows pale; the burghers turn their eyes towards heaven; all await God's punishment; all tremble except Violence on the steps of the throne and the king who is his servant.

I wish that the artist had lived long enough to take me down to the harbor of Visby and let me see those same burghers, when they followed the departing fleet with their eyes. They cry curses out over the waves. "Destroy them!" they cry. "Destroy them! Oh sea, our friend, take back our treasures! Open thy choking depths under the ungodly, under the faithless!"

And the sea murmurs a faint assent, and Violence, who stands on the royal ship, nods approvingly. "That is right," he says. "To persecute and to be persecuted, that is my law. May storm and sea destroy the pirate fleet and take to itself the treasures of my royal servant! So much the sooner it will be our lot to set out on new devastating expeditions."

The burghers on the shore turn and look up at their town. Fire has raged there; plunder has passed through it; behind broken panes gape pillaged dwellings. They see emptied streets, desecrated churches; bloody corpses are lying in the narrow courts, and women crazed by fright flee through the town. Shall they stand impotent before such things? Is there no one whom their vengeance can reach, no one whom they in their turn can torture and destroy?

God in Heaven, see! The goldsmith's house is not plundered nor burned. What does it mean? Was he in league with the enemy? Had he not the key to one of the town gates in his keeping? Oh, you daughter of Ung-Hanse, answer, what does it mean?

Far away on the royal ship Violence stands and watches his royal servant, smiling behind his visor. "Listen to the storm, Sire, listen to the storm! The gold that you have ravished will soon lie on the bottom of the sea, inaccessible to you. And look back at Visby, my noble lord! The woman whom you deceived is being led between the clergy and the soldiers to the town-wall. Can you hear the crowd following her, cursing, insulting? Look, the masons come with mortar and trowel! Look, the women come with stones! They are all bringing stones, all, all!

Oh king, if you cannot see what is passing in Visby, may you yet hear and know what is happening there. You are not of steel and iron, like Violence at your side. When the gloomy days of old age come, and you live under the shadow of death, the image of Ung-Hanse's daughter will rise in your memory.

You shall see her pale as death sink under the contempt and scorn of her people. You shall see her dragged along between the priests and the soldiers to the ringing of bells and the singing of hymns. She is already dead in the eyes of the people. She feels herself dead in her heart, killed by what she has loved. You shall see her mount in the tower, see how the stones are inserted, hear the scraping of the trowels and hear the people who hurry forward with their stones. "Oh mason, take mine, take mine! Use my stone for the work of vengeance! Let my stone help to shut Ung-Hanse's daughter in from light and air! Visby is fallen, the glorious Visby! God bless your hands, oh masons! Let me help to complete the vengeance!"

Hymns sound and bells ring as for a burial.

Oh Valdemar, King of Denmark, it will be your fate to meet death also. Then you will lie on your bed, hear and see much and suffer great pains. You shall hear that scraping of the trowels, those cries for vengeance. Where are the consecrated bells that drown the martyrdom of the soul? Where are they, with their wide, bronze throats, whose tongues cry out to God for grace for you? Where is that air trembling with harmony, which bears the soul up to God's space?

Oh help Esrom, help Soró, and you big bells of Lund!

What a gloomy story that picture told! It seemed curious and strange to come out into the park, in glowing sunshine, among living human beings.

Mamsell Fredrika

It was Christmas night, a real Christmas night.

The goblins raised the mountain roofs on lofty gold pillars and celebrated the midwinter festival. The brownies danced around the Christmas porridge in new red caps. Old gods wandered about the heavens in grey storm cloaks, and in the Österhaninge graveyard stood the horse of Hel*. He pawed with his hoof on the frozen ground; he was marking out the place for a new grave.

Not very far away, at the old manor of Årsta, Mamsell Fredrika was lying asleep. Årsta is, as everyone knows, an old haunted castle, but Mamsell Fredrika slept a calm, quiet sleep. She was old now and tired out after many weary days of work and many long journeys, – she had almost traveled round the world, – therefore she had returned to the home of her childhood to find rest.

Outside the castle sounded in the night a bold fanfare. Death mounted on a grey charger had ridden up to the castle gate. His wide scarlet cloak and his hat's proud plumes fluttered in the night wind. The stern knight sought to win an adoring heart, therefore he appeared in unusual magnificence. It is of no avail, Sir Knight, of no avail! The gate is closed, and the lady of your heart asleep. You must seek a better occasion and a more suitable hour. Watch for her when she goes to early mass, stern Sir Knight, watch for her on the church-road!

Old Mamsell Fredrika sleeps quietly in her beloved home. No one deserves more than she the sweetness of rest. Like a Christmas angel she sat but now in a circle of children, and told them of Jesus and the shepherds, told until her eyes shone, and her withered face became transfigured. Now in her old age no one noticed what Mamsell Fredrika looked like. Those who saw the little, slender figure, the tiny, delicate

* The goddess of death

hands and the kind, clever face, instantly longed to be able to preserve that sight in remembrance as the most beautiful of memories.

In Mamsell Fredrika's big room, among many relics and souvenirs, there was a little, dry bush. It was a Jericho rose, brought back by Mamsell Fredrika from the far East. Now in the Christmas night it began to blossom quite of itself. The dry twigs were covered with red buds, which shone like sparks of fire and lighted the whole room.

By the light of the sparks one saw that a small and slender but quite elderly lady sat in the big armchair and held her court. It could not be Mamsell Fredrika herself, for she lay sleeping in quiet repose, and yet it was she. She sat there and held a reception for old memories; the room was full of them. People and homes and subjects and thoughts and discussions came flying. Memories of childhood and memories of youth, love and tears, homage and bitter scorn, all came rushing towards the pale form that sat and looked at everything with a friendly smile. She had words of jest or of sympathy for them all.

At night everything takes its right size and shape. And just as then for the first time the stars of heaven are visible, one also sees much on earth that one never sees by day. Now in the light of the red buds of the Jericho rose one could see a crowd of strange figures in Mamsell Fredrika's drawing room. The hard "ma chère mère" was there, the good-natured Beata Hvardagslag, people from the East and the West, the enthusiastic Nina, the energetic, struggling Hertha in her white dress.

"Can anyone tell me why that person must always be dressed in white?" jested the little figure in the armchair when she caught sight of her.

All the memories spoke to the old woman and said: "You have seen and experienced so much; you have worked and earned so much! Are you not tired? will you not go to rest?"

"Not yet," answered the shadow in the yellow armchair. "I have still a book to write. I cannot go to rest before it is finished."

Thereupon the figures vanished. The Jericho rose went out, and the yellow armchair stood empty.

In the Österhaninge church the dead were celebrating midnight mass. One of them climbed up to the bell-tower and rang in Christmas; another went about and lighted the Christmas candles, and a third began with bony fingers to play the organ. Through the open doors others came swarming in out of the night and their graves to the bright, glowing House of the Lord. Just as they had been in life they came, only a little paler. They opened the pew doors with rattling keys and chatted and whispered as they walked up the aisle.

"They are the candles *she* has given the poor that are now shining in God's house."

"We lie warm in our graves as long as *she* gives clothes and wood to the poor."

"She has spoken so many noble words that have opened the hearts of men; those words are the keys of our pews.

"She has thought beautiful thoughts of God's love. Those thoughts raise us from our graves."

So they whispered and murmured before they sat down in the pews and bent their pale foreheads in prayer in their shrunken hands.

At Årsta someone came into Mamsell Fredrika's room and laid her hand gently on the sleeper's arm.

"Up, my Fredrika! It is time to go to the early mass."

Old Mamsell Fredrika opened her eyes and saw Agathe, her beloved sister who was dead, standing by the bed with a candle in her hand. She recognized her, for she looked just as she had done on earth. Mamsell Fredrika was not afraid; she rejoiced only at seeing her loved one, at whose side she longed to sleep the everlasting sleep.

She rose and dressed herself with all speed. There was no time for conversation; the carriage stood before the door. The others must have gone already, for no one but Mamsell Fredrika and her dead sister were moving in the house.

"Do you remember, Fredrika," said the sister, as they sat in the carriage and drove quickly to the church, "do you remember how you always in the old days expected some knight to carry you off on the road to church?"

"I am still expecting it," said old Mamsell Fredrika, and laughed. "I never ride in this carriage without looking out for my knight."

Even though they hurried, they came too late. The priest stepped down from the pulpit as they entered the church, and the closing hymn began. Never had Mamsell Fredrika heard such a beautiful song. It was as if both earth and heaven joined in, in the song; as if every bench and stone and board had sung too.

She had never seen the church so crowded: on the communion table and on the pulpit steps sat people; they stood in the aisles, they thronged in the pews, and outside the whole road was packed with people who could not enter. The sisters, however, found places; for them the crowd moved aside.

"Fredrika," said her sister, "look at the people!"

And Mamsell Fredrika looked and looked.

Then she perceived that she, like the woman in the saga, had come to a mass of the dead. She felt a cold shiver pass down her back, but it happened, as often before, she felt more curious than frightened.

She saw now who were in the church. There were none but women there: grey, bent forms, with circular capes and faded mantillas, with hats of faded splendor and turned or threadbare dresses. She saw an unheard-of number of wrinkled faces, sunken mouths, dim eyes and shriveled hands, but not a single hand which wore a plain gold ring.

Yes, Mamsell Fredrika understood it now. It was all the old maids who had passed away in the land of Sweden who were keeping midnight mass in the Österhaninge church.

Her dead sister leaned towards her.

"Sister, do you repent of what you have done for these your sisters?"

"No," said Mamsell Fredrika. "What have I to be glad for if not that it has been bestowed upon me to work for them? I once sacrificed my position as an authoress to them. I am glad that I knew what I sacrificed and yet did it."

"Then you may stay and hear more," said the sister.

At the same moment someone was heard to speak far away in the choir, a mild but distinct voice.

"My sisters," said the voice, "our pitiable race, our ignorant and despised race will soon exist no more. God has willed that we shall die out from the earth.

"Dear friends, we shall soon be only a legend. The old Mamsells' measure is full. Death rides about on the road to the church to meet the last one of us. Before the next midnight mass she will be dead, the last old Mamsell.

"Sisters, sisters! We are the lonely ones of the earth, the neglected ones at the feast, the unappreciated workers in the homes. We are met with scorn and indifference. Our way is weary and our name is ridicule.

"But God has had mercy upon us.

"To *one* of us He gave power and genius. To one of us He gave never-failing goodness. To one of us He gave the glorious gift of eloquence. She was everything we ought to have been. She threw light on our dark fate. She was the servant of the homes, as we had been, but she offered her gifts to a thousand homes. She was the caretaker of the sick, as we had been, but she struggled with the terrible epidemic of habits of former days. She told her stories to thousands of children. She lead her poor friends in every land. She gave from fuller hands than we and with a warmer spirit. In her heart dwelt none of our bitterness, for she has loved it away. Her glory has been that of a queen's. She has been offered the treasures of gratitude by millions of hearts. Her word has weighed heavily in the great questions of mankind. Her name has sounded through the new and the old world. And yet she is only an old Mamsell.

"She has transfigured our dark fate. Blessings on her name!"

The dead joined in, in a thousandfold echo: "Blessings on her name!"

"Sister," whispered Mamsell Fredrika, "can you not forbid them to make me, poor, sinful being, proud?"

"But, sisters, sisters," continued the voice, "she has turned against our race with all her great power. At her cry for freedom and work for all, the old, despised livers on charity have died out. She has broken down the tyranny that fenced in childhood. She has stirred young girls towards the wide activity of life. She has put an end to loneliness, to ignorance, to joylessness. No unhappy, despised old Mamsells without aim or purpose in life will ever exist again; none such as we have been."

Again resounded the echo of the shades, merry as a hunting-song in the wood which is sung by a happy throng of children: "Blessed be her memory!"

Thereupon the dead swarmed out of the church, and Mamsell Fredrika wiped away a tear from the corner of her eye.

"I will not go home with you," said her dead sister. "Will you not stop here now also?"

"I should like to, but I cannot. There is a book which I must make ready first."

"Well, good-night then, and beware of the knight of the church road," said her dead sister, and smiled roguishly in her old way.

Then Mamsell Fredrika drove home. All Årsta still slept, and she went quietly to her room, lay down and slept again.

A few hours later she drove to the real early mass. She drove in a closed carriage, but she let down the window to look at the stars; it is possible too that she, as of old, was looking for her knight.

And there he was; he sprang forward to the window of the carriage. He sat his prancing charger magnificently. His scarlet cloak fluttered in the wind. His pale face was stern, but beautiful.

"Will you be mine?" he whispered.

She was transported in her old heart by the lofty figure with the waving plumes. She forgot that she needed to live a year yet.

"I am ready," she whispered.

"Then I will come and fetch you in a week at your father's house."

He bent down and kissed her, and then he vanished; she began to shiver and tremble under Death's kiss.

A little later Mamsell Fredrika sat in the church, in the same place where she had sat as a child. Here she forgot both the knight and the ghosts, and sat smiling in quiet delight at the thought of the revelation of the glory of God.

But either she was tired because she had not slept the whole night, or the warmth and the closeness and the smell of the candles had a soporific effect on her as on many another.

She fell asleep, only for a second; she absolutely could not help it.

Perhaps, too, God wished to open to her the gates of the land of dreams.

In that single second when she slept, she saw her stern father, her lovely, beautifully-dressed mother, and the ugly, little Petrea sitting in the church. And the soul of the child was compressed by an anguish greater than has ever been felt by a grown person. The priest stood in the pulpit and spoke of the stern, avenging God, and the child sat pale and trembling, as if the words had been axe-blows and had gone through its heart.

"Oh, what a God, what a terrible God!"

In the next second she was awake, but she trembled and shuddered, as after the kiss of death on the church-road. Her heart was once more caught in the wild grief of her childhood.

She wished to hurry from the church. She must go home and write her book, her glorious book on the God of peace and love.

Nothing else that can be deemed worth mentioning happened to Mamsell Fredrika before New Year's night. Life and death, like day and night, reigned in quiet concord over the earth during the last week of the year, but when New Year's night came, Death took his scepter and announced that now old Mamsell Fredrika should belong to him.

Had they but known it, all the people of Sweden would certainly have prayed a common prayer to God to be allowed to keep their purest spirit, their warmest heart. Many homes in many lands where she had left loving hearts would have watched with despair and grief. The poor, the sick and the needy would have forgotten their own wants to remember hers, and all the children who had grown up blessing her work would have clasped their hands to pray for one more year for their best friend.

One year, that she might make all fully clear and put the finishing-touch on her life's work.

For Death was too prompt for Mamsell Fredrika.

There was a storm outside on that New Year's night; there was a storm within her soul. She felt all the agony of life and death coming to a crisis.

"Anguish!" she sighed, "anguish!"

But the anguish gave way, and peace came, and she whispered softly: "The love of Christ – the best love--the peace of God – the everlasting light!"

Yes, that was what she would have written in her book, and perhaps much else as beautiful and wonderful. Who knows? Only one thing we know, that books are forgotten, but such a life as hers never is.

The old prophetess's eyes closed and she sank into visions.

Her body struggled with death, but she did not know it. Her family sat weeping about her deathbed, but she did not see them. Her spirit had begun its flight.

Dreams became reality to her and reality dreams. Now she stood, as she had already seen herself in the visions of her youth, waiting at the gates of heaven with innumerable hosts of the dead round about her. And heaven opened. He, the only one, the Savior, stood in its open gates. And his infinite love woke in the waiting spirits and in her a longing to fly to his embrace, and their longing lifted them and her, and they floated as if on wings upwards, upwards.

The next day there was mourning in the land; mourning in wide parts of the earth.

Fredrika Bremer was dead.

The Romance of a Fisherman's Wife

On the outer edge of the fishing-village stood a little cottage on a low mound of white sea sand. It was not built in line with the even, neat, conventional houses that enclosed the wide green place where the brown fish-nets were dried, but seemed as if forced out of the row and pushed on one side to the sand-hills. The poor widow who had erected it had been her own builder, and she had made the walls of her cottage lower than those of all the other cottages and its steep thatched roof higher than any other roof in the fishing-village. The floor lay deep down in the ground. The window was neither high nor wide, but nevertheless it reached from the cornice to the level of the earth. There had been no space for a chimney-breast in the one narrow room and she had been obliged to add a small, square projection. The cottage had not, like the other cottages, its fenced-in garden with gooseberry bushes and twining morning-glories and elder-bushes half suffocated by burdocks. Of all the vegetation of the fishing-village, only the burdocks had followed the cottage to the sand-hill. They were fine enough in summer with their fresh, dark-green leaves and prickly baskets filled with bright, red flowers. But towards the autumn, when the prickles had hardened and the seeds had ripened, they grew careless about their looks, and stood hideously ugly and dry with their torn leaves wrapped in a melancholy shroud of dusty cobwebs.

The cottage never had more than two owners, for it could not hold up that heavy roof on its walls of reeds and clay for more than two generations. But as long as it stood, it was owned by poor widows. The second widow who lived there delighted in watching the burdocks, especially in the autumn, when they were dried and broken. They recalled her who had built the cottage. She too had been shriveled and dry and had had the power to cling fast and adhere, and all her strength had been used for her child, whom she had needed to help on in the world. She, who now sat there alone, wished both to weep and to laugh at the thought of it. If the old woman had not had a burrlike nature, how different everything would have been! But who knows if it would have been better?

The lonely woman often sat musing on the fate which had brought her to this spot on the coast of Skone, to the narrow inlet and among these quiet people. For she was born in a Norwegian seaport which lay on a narrow strip of land between rushing falls and the open sea, and although her means were small after the death of her father, a merchant, who left his family in poverty, still she was used to life and progress. She used to tell her story to herself over and over again, just as one often reads through an obscure book in order to try to discover its meaning.

The first thing of note which had happened to her was when, one evening on the way home from the dressmaker with whom she worked, she had been attacked by two sailors and rescued by a third. The latter fought for her at peril of his life and afterwards went home with her. She took him in to her mother and sisters, and told them excitedly what he had done. It was as if life had acquired a new value for her, because another had dared so much to defend it. He had been immediately well received by her family and asked to come again as soon and as often as he could.

His name was Börje Nilsson, and he was a sailor on the Swedish lugger "Albertina." As long as the boat lay in the harbor, he came almost every day to her home, and they could soon no longer believe that he was only a common sailor. He shone always in a clean, turned-down collar and wore a sailor suit of fine cloth. Natural and frank, he showed himself among them, as if he had been used to move in the same class as they. Without his ever having said it in so many words, they got the impression that he was from a respectable home, the only son of a rich widow, but that his unconquerable love for a sailor's profession had made him take a place before the mast, so that his mother should see that he was in earnest. When he had passed his examination, she would certainly get him his own ship.

The lonely family who had drawn away from all their former friends, received him without the slightest suspicion. And he described with a light heart and fluent tongue his home with its high, pointed roof, the great open fireplace in the dining room and the little leaded glass panes. He also painted the silent streets of his native town and the long rows of even houses, built in the same style, against which his home, with its irregular buttresses and terraces, made a pleasant contrast. And his listeners believed that he had come from one of those old burgher houses with carved gables and with overhanging second stories, which give such a strong impression of wealth and venerable age.

Soon enough she saw that he cared for her. And that gave her mother and sisters great joy. The young, rich Swede came as if to raise them all up from their poverty. Even if she had not loved him, which she did, she would never have had a thought of saying no to his proposal. If she had had a father or a grown-up brother, he could have found out about the stranger's extraction and position, but neither she nor her mother thought of making any inquiries. Afterwards she saw how they had actually forced him to lie. In the beginning, he had let them imagine great ideas about his wealth without any evil intention, but when he understood how glad they were over it, he had not dared to speak the truth for fear of losing her.

Before he left they were betrothed, and when the lugger came again, they were married. It was a disappointment for her that he also on his return appeared as a sailor, but he had been bound by his contract. He had no greetings either from his mother. She had expected him to make another choice, but she would be so glad, he said, if she would once see Astrid. – In spite of all his lies, it would have been an easy matter to see that he was a poor man, if they had only chosen to use their eyes.

The captain offered her his cabin if she would like to make the journey in his vessel, and the offer was accepted with delight. Börje was almost exempt from all work, and sat most of the time on the deck, talking to his wife. And now he gave her the happiness of fancy, such as he himself had lived on all his life. The more he thought of that little house which lay half buried in the sand, so much the higher he raised that palace which he would have liked to offer her. He let her in thought glide into a harbor which was adorned with flags and flowers in honor of Börje Nilsson's bride. He let her hear the mayor's speech of greeting. He let her drive under a triumphal arch, while the eyes of men followed her and the women grew pale with envy. And he led her into the stately home, where bowing, silvery-haired servants stood drawn up along the side of the broad stairway and where the table laden for the feast groaned under the old family silver.

When she discovered the truth, she supposed at first that the captain had been in league with Börje to deceive her, but afterwards she found that it was not so. They were accustomed on board the boat to speak of Börje as of a great man. It was their greatest joke to talk quite seriously of his riches and his fine family. They thought that Börje had told her the truth, but that she joked with him, as they all did, when she talked about his big house. So it happened that when the lugger cast anchor in the harbor which lay nearest to Börje's home, she still did not know but that she was the wife of a rich man.

Börje got a day's leave to conduct his wife to her future home and to start her in her new life. When they were landed on the quay, where the flags were to have fluttered and the crowds to have rejoiced in honor of the newly-married couple, only emptiness and calm reigned there, and Börje noticed that his wife looked about her with a certain disappointment.

"We have come too soon," he had said. "The journey was such an unusually quick one in this fine weather. So we have no carriage here either, and we have far to go, for the house lies outside the town."

"That makes no difference, Börje," she had answered. "It will do us good to walk, after having been quiet so long on board."

And so they began their walk, that walk of horror, of which she could not think even in her old age without moaning in agony and wringing her hands in pain. They went along the broad, empty streets, which she instantly recognized from his description. She felt as if she met with old friends both in the dark church and in the even houses of timber and brick; but where were the carved gables and marble steps with the high railing?

Börje had nodded to her as if he had guessed her thoughts. "It is a long way still," he had said.

If he had only been merciful and at once killed her hope. She loved him so then. If he of his own accord had told her everything, there would never have been any sting in her soul against him. But when he saw her pain at being deceived, and yet went on misleading her, that had hurt her too bitterly. She had never really forgiven him that. She could of course say to herself that he had wanted to take her with him as far as possible so that she would not be able to run away from him, but his deceit created such a deadly coldness in her that no love could entirely thaw it.

They went through the town and came out on the adjoining plain. There stretched several rows of dark moats and high, green ramparts, remains from the time when the town had been fortified, and at the point where they all gathered around a fort, she saw some ancient buildings and big, round towers. She cast a shy look towards them, but Börje turned off to the mounds which followed the shore.

"This is a shorter way," he said, for she seemed to be surprised that there was only a narrow path to follow.

He had become very taciturn. She understood afterwards that he had not found it so merry as he had fancied, to come with a wife to the miserable little house in the fishing village. It did not seem so fine now to bring home a better man's child. He was anxious about what she would do when she should know the truth.

"Börje," she said at last, when they had followed the shelving, sandy hillocks for a long while, "where are we going?"

He lifted his band and pointed towards the fishing-village, where his mother lived in the house on the sand-hill. But she believed that he meant one of the beautiful country-seats which lay on the edge of the plain, and was again glad.

They climbed down into the empty cow-pastures, and there all her uneasiness returned. There, where every tuft, if one can only see it, is clothed with beauty and variety, she saw merely an ugly field. And the wind, which is ever shifting there, swept whistling by them and whispered of misfortune and treachery.

Börje walked faster and faster, and at last they reached the end of the pasture and entered the fishing village. She, who at the last had not dared to ask herself any questions, took courage again. Here again was a uniform row of houses, and this one she recognized Even better than that in the town. Perhaps, perhaps he had not lied.

Her expectations were so reduced that she would have been glad from the heart if she could have stopped at any of the neat little houses, where flowers and white curtains showed behind shining windowpanes. She grieved that she had to go by them.

Then she saw suddenly, just at the outer edge of the fishing-village, one of the most wretched of hovels, and it seemed to her as if she had already seen it with her mind's eye before she actually had a glimpse of it.

"Is it here?" he said, and stopped just at the foot of the little sand-hill.

He bent his head imperceptibly and went on towards the little cottage.

"Wait," she called after him, "we must talk this over before I go into your home. You have lied," she went on, threateningly, when he turned to her. "You have deceived me worse than if you were my worst enemy. Why have you done it?"

"I wanted you for my wife," he answered, with a low, trembling voice.

"If you had only deceived me within bounds! Why did you make everything so fine and rich? What did you have to do with man-servants and triumphal arches and all the other magnificence? Did you think that I was so devoted to money? Did you not see that I cared enough for you to go anywhere with you? That you could believe you needed to deceive me! That you could have the heart to keep up your lies to the very last!"

"Will you not come in and speak to my mother?" he said, helplessly.

"I do not intend to go in there."

"Are you going home?"

"How can I go home? How could I cause them there at home such sorrow as to return, when they believe me happy and rich? But with you I will not stay either. For one who is willing to work there is always a livelihood."

"Stop!" he begged. "I did it only to win you."

"If you had told me the truth, I would have stayed."

"If I had been a rich man, who had pretended to be poor, then you would have stayed."

She shrugged her shoulders and turned to go, when the door of the cottage opened and Börje's mother came out. She was a little, dried-up old woman with few teeth and many wrinkles, but not so old in years or in feelings as in looks.

She had heard a part and guessed a part, for she knew what they were quarreling about. "Well," she said, "that is a fine daughter-in-law you have got me, Börje. And you have been deceiving again, I can hear." But to Astrid she came and patted her kindly on the cheek. "Come in with me, you poor child! I know that you are tired and worn out. This is my house. He is not allowed to come in here. But you come. Now you are my daughter, and I cannot let you go to strangers, do you understand?"

She caressed her daughter-in-law and chatted to her and drew and pushed her quite imperceptibly forward to the door. Step by step she lured her on, and at last got her inside the house; but Börje she shut out. And there, within, the old woman began to ask who she was and how it had all happened. And she wept over her and made her weep over herself. The old woman was merciless about her son. She, Astrid, did right; she could not stay with such a man. It was true that he was in the habit of lying, it was really true.

She told her how it had been with her son. He had been so fair in face and limbs, even when he was small, that she had always marveled that he was a poor man's child. He was like a little prince gone astray. And ever after it had always seemed as if he had not been in his right place. He saw everything on such a large scale. He could not see things as they were, when it concerned himself. His mother had wept many a time on that account. But never before had he done any harm with his lies. Here, where he was known, they only laughed at him. – But now he must have been so terribly tempted. Did she really not think, she, Astrid, that it was wonderful how the fisher boy had been able to deceive them? He had always known so much about wealth, as if he had been born to it. It must be that he had come into the world in the wrong place. See, that was another proof, – he had never thought of choosing a wife in his own station.

"Where will he sleep tonight?" asked Astrid, suddenly.

"I imagine he will lie outside on the sand. He will be too anxious to go away from here."

"I suppose it is best for him to come in," said Astrid.

"Dearest child, you cannot want to see him. He can get along out there if I give him a blanket."

She let him actually sleep out on the sand that night, thinking it best for Astrid not to see him. And with her she talked and talked, and kept her, not by force, but by cleverness, not by persuasion, but by real goodness.

But when she had at last succeeded in keeping her daughter-in-law for her son, and had got the young people reconciled, and had taught Astrid that her vocation in life was just to be Börje Nilsson's wife and to make him as happy as she could, – and that had not been the work of one evening, but of many days, – then the old woman had laid herself down to die.

And in that life, with its faithful solicitude for her son, there was some meaning, thought Börje Nilsson's wife.

But in her own life she saw no meaning. Her husband was drowned after a few years of married life, and her one child died young. She had not been able to make any change in her husband. She had not been able to teach him earnestness and truth. It was rather in her the change showed, after she had been more and more with the fishing people. She would never see any of her own family, for she was ashamed that she now resembled in everything a fisherman's wife. If it had only been of any use! If she, who lived by mending the fishermen's nets, knew why she clung so to life! If she had made anyone happy or had improved anybody!

It never occurred to her to think that she who considers her life a failure because she has done no good to others, perhaps by that thought of humility has saved her own soul.

His Mother's Portrait

None of the hundred houses of the fishing-village, where each is exactly like the other in size and shape, where all have just as many windows and as high chimneys, lived old Mattsson, the pilot.

In all the rooms of the fishing-village there is the same sort of furniture, on all the windowsills stand the same kinds of flowers, in all the corner-cupboards are the same collections of sea-shells and coral, on all the walls hang the same pictures. And it is a fixed old custom that all the inhabitants of the fishing-village live the same life. Since Mattsson, the pilot, had grown old, he had conformed carefully to the conditions and customs; his house, his rooms and his mode of living were like everybody else's.

On the wall over the bed old Mattsson had a picture of his mother. One night he dreamed that the portrait stepped down from its frame, placed itself in front of him and said with a loud voice: "You must marry, Mattsson."

Old Mattsson then began to make clear to his mother that it was impossible. He was seventy years old. – But his mother's portrait merely repeated with even greater emphasis: "You must marry, Mattsson."

Old Mattsson had great respect for his mother's portrait. It had been his adviser on many debatable occasions, and he had always done well by obeying it. But this time he did not quite understand its behavior. It seemed to him as if the picture was acting in opposition to its already acknowledged opinions. Although he was lying there and dreaming, he remembered distinctly and clearly what had happened the first time he wished to be married. Just as he was dressing as a bridegroom, the nail gave way on which the picture hung and it fell to the floor. He understood then that the portrait wished to warn him against the marriage, but he did not obey it. He soon found that the portrait had been right. His short married life was very unhappy.

The second time he dressed as a bridegroom the same thing happened. The portrait fell to the ground as before, and he did not dare again to disobey it. He ran away from bride and wedding and traveled round the world several times before he dared come home again. – And now the picture stepped down from the wall and commanded him to marry! However good and obedient he was, he allowed himself to think that it was making a fool of him.

But his mother's portrait, which looked out with the grimmest face that sharp winds and salt sea-foam could carve, stood solemnly as before. And with a voice which had been exercised and strengthened for many years by offering fish in the town marketplace, it repeated: "You must marry, Mattsson."

Old Mattsson then asked his mother's portrait to consider what kind of a community it was they lived in.

All the hundred houses of the fishing-village had pointed roofs and whitewashed walls; all the boats of the fishing-village were of the same build and rig. No one there ever did anything unusual. His mother would have been the first to oppose such a marriage if she had been alive. His mother had held by habits and customs. And it was not the habit and custom of the fishing-village for old men of seventy years to marry.

His mother's picture stretched out her beringed hand and positively commanded him to obey. There had always been something excessively awe-inspiring in his mother when she came in her black silk dress with many flounces. The big, shining gold brooch, the heavy, rattling gold chain had always frightened him. If she had worn her market-clothes, in a striped head-cloth and with an oilcloth apron, covered with fish-scales and fish eyes, he would not have been quite so overawed by her. The end of it was that he promised to get married. And then his mother's portrait crept up into the frame again.

The next morning old Mattsson woke in great trouble. It never occurred to him to disobey his mother's portrait; it knew of course what was best for him. But he shuddered nevertheless at the time that was now coming.

The same day he made an offer of marriage to the plainest daughter of the poorest fisherman, a little creature, whose head was drawn down between her shoulders and who had a projecting under-jaw. The parents said yes, and the day when he was to go to the town and publish the bans was appointed.

The road from the fishing-village to the town passes over windy marshes and swampy cow-pastures. It is two miles long, and there is a tradition that the inhabitants of the fishing-village are so rich that they could pave it with shining silver coins. It would give the road a strange attraction. Glimmering like a fish's belly, it would wind with its white scales through clumps of sedge and pools filled with water-bugs and melancholy bullfrogs. The daisies and almond-blossoms which adorn that forsaken ground would be mirrored in the shining silver coins; thistles would stretch out protecting thorns over them, and the wind would find a ringing sounding-board when it played on the thatched roof of the cow-barns and on telephone-wires.

Perhaps old Mattsson would have found some comfort if he could have set his heavy sea boots on ringing silver, for it is certain that he for a time had to go that way oftener than he liked.

He had not had "clean papers." The bans could not be published. It came from his having run away from his bride the last time. Some time passed before the clergyman could write to the consistory about him and get permission for him to contract a new marriage.

As long as this time of waiting lasted, old Mattsson came to the town every week. He sat by the door of the pastor's room and remained there in silent expectation until all had spoken in turn. Then he rose and asked if the clergyman had anything for him. No, he had nothing.

The pastor was amazed at the power that all-conquering love had acquired over that old man. There he sat in a thick, knitted jersey, high sea-boots and weather-beaten sou'wester with a sharp, clever face and long, grey hair, and waited for permission to get married. The clergyman thought it strange that the old fisherman should have been seized by so eager a longing.

"You are in a hurry with this marriage, Mattsson," said the clergyman.

"Oh yes, it is best to get it done soon."

"Could you not just as well give up the whole thing? You are no longer young, Mattsson."

The clergyman must not be too surprised. He knew well enough that he was too old, but he was obliged to be married. There was no help for it.

So he came again week after week for a half year, until at last the permission came.

During all that time old Mattsson was a persecuted man. Round the green drying-place, where the brown fish-nets were hung out, along the cemented walls by the harbor, at the fish-tables in the market, where cod and crabs were sold, and far out in the sound among the shoals of herring, raged a storm of wonder and laughter.

"So he is going to be married, he, Mattsson, who ran away from his own wedding!"

Neither bride nor groom were spared.

But the worst thing for him was that no one could laugh more at the whole thing than he himself. No one could find it more ridiculous. His mother's portrait was driving him mad.

It was the afternoon of the first time of asking. Old Mattsson, still pursued by talk and wonderings, went out on the long breakwater as far as the whitewashed lighthouse, in order to be alone. He found his betrothed there. She sat and wept.

He asked her whether she would have liked someone else better. She sat and pried little bits of mortar from the lighthouse wall and threw them into the water, answering nothing at first.

"Was there nobody you liked?"

"Oh no, of course not."

It is very beautiful out by the lighthouse. The clear water of the sound laps about it. The low-lying shore, the little uniform houses of the fishing-village, and the distant town are all shining in wonderful beauty. Out of the soft mist that hovers on the western horizon a fishing-boat comes gliding now and again. Tacking boldly, it steers towards the harbor. The water roars gaily past its bow as it shoots in through the narrow harbor entrance. The sail drops silently at the same moment. The fishermen swing their hats in joyous greeting, and on the bottom of the boat lies the glittering spoil.

A boat came into the harbor while old Mattsson stood out by the lighthouse. A young man sitting at the tiller lifted his hat and nodded to the girl. The old man saw that her eyes were shining.

"Well," he thought, "have you fallen in love with the handsomest young fellow in the fishing-village? Yes, you will never get him. You may just as well marry me as wait for him."

He saw that he could not escape his mother's picture. If the girl had cared for anyone whom there was any possibility of getting, he would have had a good motive to be rid of the whole business. But now it was useless to set her free.

A fortnight later was the wedding, and a few days after came the big November gale. One of the boats of the fishing-village was swept out into the sound. It had neither rudder nor masts, so that it was quite unmanageable. Old Mattsson and five others were on board, and they drifted about without food for two days. When they were rescued, they were in a state of exhaustion from hunger and cold. Everything in the boat was covered with ice, and their wet clothes were stiff. Old Mattsson was so chilled that he never was well again. He lay ill for two years; then death came.

Many thought that it was strange that his idea of marrying came just before the unlucky adventure, for the little woman he had got took good care of him. What would he have done if he had been alone when lying so helpless? The whole fishing-village acknowledged that he had never done anything more sensible than marrying, and the little woman won great consideration for the tenderness with which she took care of her husband.

"She will have no trouble in marrying again," people said.

Old Mattsson told his wife, every day while he lay ill, the story of the portrait.

"You must take it when I am dead, just as you must take everything of mine," he said.

"Do not speak of such things."

"And you must listen to my mother's portrait when the young men propose to you. Truly there is no one in the whole fishing-village who understands getting married better than that picture."

A Fallen King

Mine was the kingdom of fancy, now I am a fallen king.

– Snoilsky

The wooden shoes clattered in uneasy measure on the pavements. The street boys hurried by. They shouted, they whistled. The houses shook, and from the courts the echo rushed out like a chained dog from his kennel.

Faces appeared behind the windowpanes. Had anything happened? Was anything going on? The noise passed on towards the suburbs. The servant girls hastened after, following the street boys. They clasped their hands and screamed: "Preserve us, preserve us! Is it murder, is it fire?" No one answered. The clattering was heard far away.

After the maids came hurrying wise matrons of the town. They asked: "What is it? What is disturbing the morning calm? Is it a wedding? Is it a funeral? Is it a conflagration? What is the watchman doing? Shall the town burn up before he begins to sound the alarm?"

The whole crowd stopped before the shoemaker's little house in the suburbs, the little house that had vines climbing about the doors and windows, and in front, between street and house, a yard-wide garden. Summer-houses of straw, arbors fit for a mouse, paths for a kitten. Everything in the best of order! Peas and beans, roses and lavender, a mouthful of grass, three gooseberry bushes and an apple tree.

The street boys who stood nearest stared and consulted. Through the shining, black windowpanes their glances penetrated no further than to the white lace curtains. One of the boys climbed up on the vines and pressed his face against the pane. "What do you see?" whispered the others. "What do you see?" The shoemaker's shop and the shoemaker's bench, grease-pots and bundles of leather, lasts and pegs, rings and straps. "Don't you see anybody?" He sees the apprentice, who is repairing a shoe. Nobody else, nobody else? Big, black flies crawl over the pane and make his sight uncertain. "Do you see nobody except the apprentice?" Nobody. The master's chair is empty. He looked once, twice, three times; the master's chair was empty.

The crowd stood still, guessing and wondering. So it was true; the old shoemaker had absconded. Nobody would believe it. They stood and waited for a sign. The cat came out on the steep roof. He stretched out his claws and slid down to the gutter. Yes, the master was away, the cat could hunt as he pleased. The sparrows fluttered and chirped, quite helpless.

A white chicken looked round the corner of the house. He was almost full-grown. His comb shone red as wine. He peered and spied, crowed and called. The hens came, a row of white hens at full speed, bodies rocking, wings fluttering, yellow legs like drumsticks. The hens hopped among the stacked peas. Battles began. Envy broke out. A hen fled with a full pea-pod. Two cocks pecked her in the neck. The cat left the sparrow nests to look on. Plump, there he fell down in the midst of the flock. The hens fled in a long, scurrying line. The crowd thought: "It must be true that the shoemaker has run away. One can see by the cat and the hens that the master is away."

The uneven street, muddy from the autumn rains, resounded with talk. Doors stood open, windows swung. Heads were put together in wondering whisperings. "He has run off." The people whispered, the sparrows chirped, the wooden shoes clattered: "He has run away. The old shoemaker has run away. The owner of the little house, the young wife's husband, the father of the beautiful child, he has run away. Who can understand it? who can explain it?"

There is an old song: "Old husband in the cottage; young lover in the wood; wife, who runs away, child who cries; home without a mistress." The song is old. It is often sung. Everybody understands it.

This was a new song. The old man was gone. On the workshop table lay his explanation, that he never meant to come back. Beside it a letter had also lain. The wife had read it, but no one else.

The young wife was in the kitchen. She was doing nothing. The neighbors went backwards and forwards, arranging busily, set out the cups, made up the fire, boiled the coffee, wept a little and wiped away the tears with the dish-towel.

The good women of the quarter sat stiffly about the walls. They knew what was suitable in a house of mourning. They kept silent by force, mourned by force. They celebrated their holiday by supporting the forsaken wife in her grief. Coarse hands lay quiet in their laps, weather-beaten skin lay in deep wrinkles, thin lips were pressed together over toothless jaws.

The wife sat among the bronze-hued women, gently blonde, with a sweet face like a dove. She did not weep, but she trembled. She was so afraid, that the fear was almost killing her. She bit her teeth together, so that no one should hear how they chattered. When steps were heard, when the clattering sounded, when someone spoke to her, she started up.

She sat with her husband's letter in her pocket. She thought of now one line in it and now another. There stood: "I can bear no longer to see you both." And in another place: "I know now that you and Erikson mean to elope." And again: "You shall not do that, for people's evil talk would make you unhappy. I shall disappear, so that you can get a divorce and be properly married. Erikson is a good workman and can support you well." Then farther down: "Let people say what they will about me. I am content if only they do not think any evil of you, for you could not bear it."

She did not understand it. She had not meant to deceive him. Even if she had liked to chat with the young apprentice, what had her husband to do with that? Love is an illness, but it is not mortal. She had meant to bear it through life with patience. How had her husband discovered her most secret thoughts?

She was tortured at the thought of him! He must have grieved and brooded. He had wept over his years. He had raged over the young man's strength and spirits. He had trembled at the whisperings, at the smiles, at the hand pressures. In burning madness, in glowing jealousy, he had made it into a whole elopement history, of which there was as yet nothing.

She thought how old he must have been that night when he went. His back was bent, his hands shook. The agony of many long nights had made him so. He had gone to escape that existence of passionate doubting.

She remembered other lines in the letter: "It is not my intention to destroy your character. I have always been too old for you." And then another: "You shall always be respected and honored. Only be silent, and all the shame will fall on me!"

The wife felt deeper and deeper remorse. Was it possible that people would be deceived? Would it do to lie so too before God? Why did she sit in the cottage, pitied like a mourning mother, honored like a bride on her wedding day? Why was it not she who was homeless, friendless, despised? How can such things be? How can God let himself be so deceived?

Over the great dresser hung a little bookcase. On the top shelf stood a big book with brass clasps. Behind those clasps was hidden the story of a man and a woman who lied before God and men. "Who has suggested to you, woman, to do such things? Look, young men stand outside to lead you away."

The woman stared at the book, listened for the young men's footsteps. She trembled at every knock, shuddered at every step. She was ready to stand up and confess, ready to fall down and die.

The coffee was ready. The women glided sedately forward to the table. They filled their cups, took a lump of sugar in their mouths and began to sip their boiling coffee, silently and decently, the wives of mechanics first, the scrub-women last. But the wife did not see what was going on. Remorse made her quite beside herself. She had a vision. She sat at night out in a freshly plowed field. Round about her sat great birds with mighty wings and pointed beaks. They were grey, scarcely perceptible against the grey ground, but they held watch over her. They were passing sentence upon her. Suddenly they flew up and sank down over her head. She saw their sharp claws, their pointed beaks, their beating wings coming nearer and nearer. It was like a deadly rain of steel. She bent her head and knew that she must die. But when they came near, quite near to her, she had to look up. Then she saw that the grey birds were all these old women.

One of them began to speak. She knew what was proper, what was fitting in a house of mourning. They had now been silent long enough. But the wife started up as from a blow. What did the woman mean to say? "You, Matts Wik's wife, Anna Wik, confess! You have lied long enough before God and before us. We are your judges. We will judge you and rend you to pieces."

No, the woman began to speak of husbands. And the others chimed in, as the occasion demanded. What was said was not in the husbands' praise. All the evil husbands had done was dragged forward. It was as consolation for a deserted wife.

Injury was heaped upon injury. Strange beings these husbands! They beat us, they drink up our money, they pawn our furniture. Why on earth had Our Lord created them?

The tongues became like dragons' fangs; they spat venom, they spouted fire. Each one added her word. Anecdotes were piled upon anecdotes. A wife fled from her home before a drunken husband. Wives slaved for idle husbands. Wives were deserted for other women. The tongues whistled like whip lashes. The misery of homes was laid bare. Long litanies were read. From the tyranny of the husband deliver us, good Lord!

Illness and poverty, the children's death, the winter's cold, trouble with the old people, everything was the husband's fault. The slaves hissed at their masters. They turned their stings against them, before whose feet they crept.

The deserted wife felt how it cut and stabbed in her ears. She dared to defend the incorrigible ones. "My husband," she said, "is good." The women started up, hissed and snorted. "He has run away. He is no better than anybody else. He, who is an old man, ought to know better than to run away from wife and child. Can you believe that he is better than the others?"

The wife trembled; she felt as if she was being dragged through prickly bramble-bushes. Her husband considered a sinner! She flushed with shame, wished to speak, but was silent. She was afraid; she had not the power. But why did God keep silent? Why did God let such things be?

If she should take the letter and read it aloud, then the stream of poison would be turned. The venom would sprinkle upon her. The horror of death came over her. She did not dare. She half wished that an insolent hand had been thrust into her pocket and had drawn out the letter. She could not give herself as a prize. Within the workshop was heard a shoemaker's hammer. Did no one hear how it hammered in triumph? She had heard that hammering and had been vexed by it the whole day. But none of the women understood it. Omniscient God, hast Thou no servant who could read hearts? She would gladly accept her sentence, if only she did not need to confess. She wished to hear someone say: "Who has given you the idea to lie before God?" She listened for the sound of the young men's footsteps in order to fall down and die.

Several years after this a divorced woman was married to a shoemaker, who had been apprentice to her husband. She had not wished it, but had been drawn to it, as a pickerel is drawn to the side of a boat when it has been caught on the line. The fisherman lets it play. He lets it rush here and there. He lets it believe it is free. But when it is tired out, when it can do no more, then he drags with a light pull, then he lifts it up and jerks it down into the bottom of the boat before it knows what it is all about.

The wife of the absconded shoemaker had dismissed her apprentice and wished to live alone. She had wished to show her husband that she was innocent. But where was her husband? Did he not care for her faithfulness. She suffered want. Her child went in rags. How long did her husband think that she could wait? She was unhappy when she had no one upon whom she could depend.

Erikson succeeded. He had a shop in the town. His shoes stood on glass shelves behind broad plate-glass windows. His workshop grew. He hired an apartment and put plush furniture in the parlor. Everything waited only for her. When she was too wearied of poverty, she came.

She was very much afraid in the beginning. But no misfortunes befell her. She became more confident as time went on and more happy. She had people's regard, and knew within herself that she had not deserved it. That kept her conscience awake, so that she became a good woman.

Her first husband, after some years, came back to the house in the suburbs. It was still his, and he settled down again there and wished to begin work. But he got no work, nor would anybody have anything to do with him. He was despised, while his wife enjoyed great honor. It was nevertheless he who had done right, and she who had done wrong.

The husband kept his secret, but it almost suffocated him. He felt how he sank, because everybody considered him bad. No one had any confidence in him, no one would trust any work to him. He took what company he could get, and learned to drink.

While he was going down hill, the Salvation Army came to the town. It hired a big hall and began its work. From the very first evening all the loafers gathered at the meetings to make a disturbance. When it had gone on for about a week, Matts Wik came too to take part in the fun.

There was a crowd in the street, a crowd in the door-way. Sharp elbows and angry tongues were there; street boys and soldiers, maids and scrub-women; peaceable police and stormy rabble. The army was new and the fashion. The well-to-do and the wharf-rats, everybody went to the Salvation Army. Within, the hall was low-studded. At the farthest end was an empty platform; unpainted benches, borrowed chairs, an uneven floor, blotches on the ceiling, lamps that smoked. The iron stove in the middle of the floor gave out warmth and coal gas. All the places were filled in a moment. Nearest the platform sat the women, demure as if in church, and back of them workmen and sewing-women. Farthest away sat the boys on one another's knees, and in the door-way there was a fight among those who could not get in.

The platform was empty. The clock had not struck, the entertainment had not begun. One whistled, one laughed. The benches were kicked to pieces. "The War-cry" flew like a kite between the groups. The public were enjoying themselves.

A side-door opened. Cold air streamed into the room. The fire flamed up. There was silence. Attentive expectation filled the hall. At last they came, three young women, carrying guitars and with faces almost hidden by broad-brimmed hats. They fell on their knees as soon as they had ascended the steps of the platform.

One of them prayed aloud. She lifted her head, but closed her eyes. Her voice cut like a knife. During the prayer there was silence. The street-boys and loafers had not yet begun. They were waiting for the confessions and the inspiring music.

The women settled down to their work. They sang and prayed, sang and preached. They smiled and spoke of their happiness. In front of them they had an audience of ruffians. They began to rise, they climbed upon the benches. A threatening noise passed through the throng. The women on the platform caught glimpses of dreadful faces through the smoky air. The men had wet, dirty clothes, which smelt badly. They spat tobacco every other second, swore with every word. Those women, who were to struggle with them, spoke of their happiness.

How brave that little army was! Ah, is it not beautiful to be brave? Is it not something to be proud of to have God on one's side? It was not worth while to laugh at them in their big hats. It was most probable that they would conquer the hard hands, the cruel faces, the blaspheming lips.

"Sing with us!" cried the Salvation Army soldiers; "sing with us! It is good to sing." They started a well-known melody. They struck their guitars and repeated the same verse over and over. They got one or two of those sitting nearest to join in, but now sounded down by the door a light street song. Notes struggled against notes, words against words, guitar against whistle. The women's strong, trained voices contested with the boys' hoarse falsetto, with the men's growling bass. When the street song was almost conquered, they began to stamp and whistle down by the door. The Salvation Army song sank like a wounded warrior. The noise was terrifying. The women fell on their knees.

They knelt as if powerless. Their eyes were closed. Their bodies rocked in silent pain. The noise died down. The Salvation Army captain began instantly: "Lord, all these Thou wilt make Thine own. We thank Thee, Lord, that Thou wilt lead them all into Thy host! We thank Thee, Lord, that it is granted to us to lead them to Thee!"

The crowd hissed, howled, screamed. It was as if all those throats had been tickled by a sharp knife. It was as if the people had been afraid to be won over, as if they had forgotten that they had come there of their own will.

But the woman continued, and it was her sharp, piercing voice which conquered. They had to hear.

"You shout and scream; the old serpent within you is twisting and raging. But that is just the sign. Blessings on the old serpent's roarings! It shows that he is tortured, that he is afraid. Laugh at us! Break our windows! Drive us away from the platform! Tomorrow you will belong to us. We shall possess the earth. How can you withstand us? How can you withstand God?"

Then the captain commanded one of her comrades to come forward and make her confession. She came smiling. She stood brave and undaunted and told the story of her sin and her conversion to the mockers. Where had that kitchen-girl learned to stand smiling under all that scorn? Some of those who had come to scoff grew pale. Where had these women found their courage and their strength? Someone stood behind them.

The third woman stepped forward. She was a beautiful child, daughter of rich parents, with a sweet, clear voice. She did not tell of herself. Her testimony was one of the usual songs.

It was like the shadow of a victory. The audience forgot itself and listened. The child was lovely to look at, sweet to hear. But when she ceased, the noise became even more dreadful. Down by the door they built a platform of benches, climbed up and confessed.

It became worse and worse in the hall. The stove became red hot, devoured air and belched heat. The respectable women on the front benches looked about for a way to escape, but there was no possibility of getting out. The soldiers on the platform perspired and wilted. They cried and prayed for strength. Suddenly a breath came through the air, a whisper reached their ear. They knew not from where, but they felt a change. God was with them. He fought for them.

To the struggle again! The captain stepped forward and lifted the Bible over her head. Stop, stop! We feel that God is working among us. A conversion is near. Help us to pray! God will give us a soul.

They fell on their knees in silent prayer. Some in the hall joined in the prayer. All felt an intense expectation. Was it true? Was something great taking place in a fellow-creature's soul, here, in their midst? Should it be granted to them to see it? Could it be influenced by these women?

For the moment the crowd was won. They were now just as eager for a miracle as lately for blasphemy. No one dared to move. All panted from excitement, but nothing happened. "O God, Thou forsakest us! Thou forsakest us, O God!"

The beautiful salvation soldier began to sing. She chose the mildest of melodies: "Oh, my beloved, wilt Thou not come soon?"

Touching as a praying child, the song entered their souls – like a caress, like a blessing.

The crowd was silent, wrapped in those notes. "Mountains and forests long, heaven and earth languish. Man, everything in the world, thirsts that you shall open your soul to the light. Then glory will spread over the earth, then the beasts will rise up from their degradation.

"Oh, my beloved, wilt thou not come soon?"

"It is not true that thou dost linger in lofty halls. In the dark wood, in miserable hovels thou dwellest. And thou wilt not come. My bright heaven does not tempt thee.

"Oh, my beloved, wilt thou not come soon?"

In the hall more and more began to sing the burden. Voice after voice joined in. They did not rightly know what words they used. The tune was enough. All their longing could sing itself free in those tones. They sang, too, down by the door. Hearts were bursting. Wills were subdued. It no longer sounded like a pitiful lament, but strong, imperative, commanding.

"Oh, my beloved, wilt thou not come soon?"

Down by the door, in the worst of the crowd, stood Matts Wik. He looked much intoxicated, but that evening he had not drunk. He stood and thought. "If I might speak, if I might speak!"

It was the strangest room he had ever seen, the most wonderful chance. A voice seemed to say to him: "These are the rushes to which you can whisper, the waves which will bear your voice."

The singers started. It was as if they had heard a lion roar in their ears. A mighty, terrible voice spoke dreadful words.

It scoffed at God. Why did men serve God? He forsook all those who served him. He had failed his own son. God helped no one.

The voice grew louder, more like a roar every minute. No one could have believed that human lungs could have such strength. No one had ever heard such ravings burst from bruised heart. All bent their heads like wanderers in the desert, when the storm beats on them.

Terrible, terrible words! They were like thundering hammer strokes against God's throne. Against Him who had tortured Job, who had let the martyrs suffer, who let those who professed his faith burn at the stake.

A few had at first tried to laugh. Some of them had thought that it was a joke. But now they heard, quaking, that it was in earnest. Already some rose up to flee to the platform. They asked the protection of the Salvation Army from him who drew down upon them the wrath of God.

The voice asked them in hissing tones what rewards they expected for their trouble in serving God. They need not count on heaven. God was not freehanded with His heaven. A man, he said, had done more good than was needed to be blessed. He had brought greater offerings than God demanded. But then he had been tempted to sin. Life is long. He paid out his hard-earned grace already in this world. He would go the way of the damned.

The speech was the terrifying north-wind, which drives the ship into the harbor. While the scoffer spoke, women rushed up to the platform. The Salvation Army soldiers' hands were embraced and kissed; they were scarcely able to receive them all. The boys and the old men praised God.

He who spoke continued. The words intoxicated him. He said to himself: "I speak, I speak, at last I speak. I tell them my secret, and yet I do not tell them." For the first time since he made the great sacrifice he was free from care.

It was a Sunday afternoon in the height of the summer. The town looked like a desert of stones, like a moon landscape. There was not a cat to be seen, nor a sparrow, hardly a fly on the sunny wall. Not a chimney smoked. There was not a breath of air in the sultry streets. The whole was only a stony field, out of which grew stone walls.

Where were the dogs and the people? Where were the young ladies in narrow skirts and wide sleeves, long gloves and red sunshades? Where were the soldiers and the fine people, the Salvation Army and the street boys?

Whither had all those gay picnickers gone in the dewy cool of the morning, all the baskets and accordions and bottles, which the steamer landed? And what had happened to the procession of Good Templars? Banners fluttered, drums thundered, boys swarmed, stamped, and hurrahed. Or what had happened to the blue awnings under which the little ones slept while father and mother pushed them solemnly up the street.

All were on their way out to the wood. They complained of the long streets. It seemed as if the stone houses followed them. At last, at last they caught a glimpse of green. And just outside of the town, where the road wound over flat, moist fields, where the song of the lark sounded loudest, where the clover steamed with honey, there lay the first of those left behind; heads in the moss, noses in the grass. Bodies bathed in sunshine and fragrance, souls refreshed with idleness and rest.

On the way to the wood toiled bicyclists and bearers of luncheon baskets. Boys came with trowels and shiny knapsacks. Girls danced in clouds of dust. Sky and banners and children and trumpets. Mechanics and their families and crowds of laborers. The rearing horses of an omnibus waved their forelegs over the crowd. A young man, half drunk, jumped up on the wheel. He was pulled down, and lay kicking on his back in the dust of the road.

In the wood a nightingale trilled and sang, piped and gurgled. The birches were not thriving, their trunks were black. The beeches built high temples, layer upon layer of streaky green. A toad sat and took aim with its tongue. It caught a fly at every shot. A hedgehog trotted about in the dried, rustling beech leaves. Dragonflies darted about with glittering wings. The people sat down around the luncheon-baskets. The piping, chirping crickets tried to make their Sunday a glad one.

Suddenly the hedgehog disappeared, terrified he rolled himself up in his prickles. The crickets crept into the grass, quite silenced. The nightingale sang as if its throat would burst. It was guitars, guitars. The Salvation Army marched forward under the beeches. The people started up from their rest under the trees. The dancing-green and croquet-ground were deserted. The swings and merry-go-rounds had an hour's rest. Everybody followed to the Salvation Army's camp. The benches filled, and listeners sat on every hillock. The army had waxed strong and powerful. About many a fair cheek was tied the Salvation Army hat. Many a strong man wore the red shirt. There was peace and order in the crowd. Bad words did not venture to pass the lips. Oaths rumbled harmlessly behind teeth. And Matts Wik, the shoemaker, the terrible blasphemer, stood now as standard-bearer by the platform. He, too, was one of the believers. The red flag caressed his grey head.

The Salvation Army soldiers had not forgotten the old man. They had him to thank for their first victory. They had come to him in his loneliness. They washed his floor and mended his clothes. They did not refuse to associate with him. And at their meetings he was allowed to speak.

Ever since he had broken his silence he was happy. He stood no longer as an enemy of God. There was a raging power in him. He was happy when he could let it out. When souls were shaken by his lion voice, he was happy.

He spoke always of himself. He always told his own story. He described the fate of the misjudged. He spoke of sacrifices of life itself, made without a hope of reward, without acknowledgment. He disguised what he related. He told his secret and yet did not tell it.

He became a poet. He had the power of winning hearts. For his sake crowds gathered in front of the Salvation Army platform. He drew them by the fantastic images which filled his diseased brain. He captivated them with the words of affecting lament, which the oppression of his heart had taught him.

Perhaps his spirit in days of old had visited this world of death and change. Perhaps he had then been a mighty skald, skillful in playing on heartstrings. But for some evil deed he had been condemned to begin again his earthly life, to live by the work of his hands, without the knowledge of the strength of his spirit. But now his grief had broken his spirit's chains. His soul was a newly released bird. Timid and confused, but still rejoicing in its freedom, it flew onward over the old battlefields.

The wild, ignorant singer, the black thrush, which had grown among starlings, listened diffidently to the words which came to his lips. Where did he get the power to compel the crowd to listen in ecstasy to his speech? Where did he get the power to force proud men down upon their knees, wringing their hands? He trembled before he began to speak. Then a quiet confidence came over him. From the inexhaustible depths of his suffering rose ever torrents of agonized words.

Those speeches were never printed. They were hunting-cries, ringing trumpet-notes, rousing, animating, terrifying, urgent; not to capture, not to give again. They were lightning flashes and rolling thunder. They shook hearts with terrible alarms. But they were transient, never could they be caught. The cataract can be measured to its last drop, the dizzy play of foam can be painted, but not the elusive, delirious, swift, growing, mighty stream of those speeches.

That day in the wood he asked the gathering if they knew how they should serve God? – as Uria served his king.

Then he, the man in the pulpit, became Uria. He rode through the desert with the letter of his king. He was alone. The solitude terrified him. His thoughts were gloomy. But he smiled when he thought of his wife. The desert became a flowering meadow when he remembered his wife. Springs gushed up from the ground at the thought of her.

His camel fell. His soul was filled with forebodings of evil. Misfortune, he thought, is a vulture, which loves the desert. He did not turn, but went onward with the king's letter. He trod upon thorns. He walked among serpents and scorpions. He thirsted and hungered. He saw caravans drag their dark length through the sands. He did not join them. He dared not seek strangers. He, who bears a royal letter, must go alone. He saw at eventide the white tents of shepherds. He was tempted, as if by his wife's smiling dwelling. He thought he saw white veils waving to him. He turned away from the tents out into solitude. Woe to him if they had stolen the letter of his king!

He hesitates when he sees searching brigands pursuing him. He thinks of the king's letter. He reads it in order to then destroy it. He reads it, and finds new courage. Stand up, warrior of Judah! He does not destroy the letter. He does not give himself up to the robbers. He fights and conquers. And so onward, onward! He bears his sentence of death through a thousand dangers. . . .

It is so God's will shall be obeyed through tortures unto death. . . .

While Wik spoke, his divorced wife stood and listened to him. She had gone out to the wood that morning, beaming and contented on her husband's arm, most matronlike, respectable in every fold. Her daughter and the apprentice carried the luncheon basket. The maid followed with the youngest child. There had been nothing but content, happiness, calm.

There they had lain in a thicket. They had eaten and drunk, played and laughed. Never a thought of the past! Conscience was as silent as a satisfied child. In the beginning, when her first husband had slunk half drunk by her window, she had felt a prick in her soul.

Then she had heard that he had become the idol of the Salvation Army. She was, therefore, quite calm. Now she had come to hear him. And she understood him. He was not speaking of Uria; he was telling about himself. He was writhing at the thought of his own sacrifice. He tore bits from his own heart and threw them out among the people. She knew that rider in the desert, that conqueror of brigands. And that unappeased agony stared at her like an open grave. . . .

Night came. The wood was deserted. Farewell, grass and flowers! Wide heaven, a long farewell! Snakes began to crawl about the tufts of grass. Turtles crept along the paths. The wood was ugly. Everybody longed to be back in the stone desert, the moon landscape. That is the place for men.

Dame Anna Erikson invited all her old friends. The mechanics' wives from the suburbs and the poorer scrub-women came to her for a cup of coffee. The same were there who had been with her on the day of her desertion. One was new, Maria Anderson, the captain of the Salvation Army.

Anna Erikson had now been many times to the Salvation Army. She had heard her husband. He always told about himself. He disguised his story. She recognized it always. He was Abraham. He was Job. He was Jeremiah, whom the people threw into a well. He was Elisha, whom the children at the wayside reviled.

That pain seemed bottomless to her. His sorrow seemed to her to borrow all voices, to make itself masks of everything it met. She did not understand that her husband talked himself well, that pleasure in his power of fancy played and smiled in him.

She had dragged her daughter with her. The daughter had not wished to go. She was serious, modest, and conscientious. Nothing of youth played in her veins. She was born old.

She had grown up in shame of her father. She walked upright, austere, as if saying: "Look, the daughter of a man who is despised! Look if my dress is soiled! Is there anything to blame in my conduct?" Her mother was proud of her. Yet sometimes she sighed. "Alas! if my daughter's hands were less white, perhaps her caresses would be warmer!"

The girl sat scornfully smiling. She despised theatricals. When her father rose up to speak, she wished to go. Her mother's hand seized hers, fast as a vice. The girl sat still. The torrent of words began to roar over her. But that which spoke to her was not so much the words as her mother's hand.

That hand writhed, convulsions passed through it. It lay in hers limp, as if dead; it caught wildly about, hot with fever. Her mother's face betrayed nothing; only her hand suffered and struggled.

The old speaker described the martyrdom of silence. The friend of Jesus lay ill. His sisters sent a message to him; but his time had not come. For the sake of God's kingdom Lazarus must die.

He now let all doubting, all slander be heaped upon Christ. He described his suffering. His own compassion tortured him. He passed through the agony of death, he as well as Lazarus. Still he had to keep silence.

Only one word had he needed to say to win back the respect of his friends. He was silent. He had to hear the lamentations of the sisters. He told them the truth in words which they did not understand. Enemies mocked at him.

And so on always more and more affecting.

Anna Erikson's hand still lay in that of her daughter. It confessed and acknowledged: "The man there bears the martyr's crown of silence. He is wrongly accused. With a word he could set himself free."

The girl followed her mother home. They went in silence. The girl's face was like stone. She was pondering, searching for everything which memory could tell her. Her mother looked anxiously at her. What did she know?

The next day Anna Erikson had her coffee party. The talk turned on the day's market, on the price of wooden shoes, on pilfering maids. The women chatted and laughed. They poured their coffee into the saucer. They were mild and unconcerned. Anna Erikson could not understand why she had been afraid of them, why she had always believed that they would judge her.

When they were provided with their second cup, when they sat delighted with the coffee trembling on the edge of their cups, and their saucers were filled with bread, she began to speak. Her words were a little solemn, but her voice was calm.

"Young people are imprudent. A girl who marries without thinking seriously of what she is doing can come to great grief. Who has met with worse than I?"

They all knew it. They had been with her and had mourned with her.

"Young people are imprudent. One holds one's tongue when one ought to speak, for shame's sake. One dares not to speak for fear of what people will say. He who has not spoken at the right time may have to repent it a whole lifetime."

They all believed that this was true.

She had heard Wik yesterday as well as many times before. Now she must tell them all something about him. An aching pain came over her when she thought of what he had suffered for her sake. Still she thought that he, who had been old, ought to have had more sense than to take her, a young girl, for his wife.

"I did not dare to say it in my youth. But he went away from me out of pity, for he thought that I wanted to have Erikson. I have his letter about it."

She read the letter aloud for them. A tear glided demurely down her cheek.

"He had seen falsely in his jealousy. Between Erikson and me there was nothing then. It was four years before we were married; but I will say it now, for Wik is too good to be misjudged. He did not run away from wife and child from light motives, but with good intention. I want this to be known everywhere. Captain Anderson will perhaps read the letter aloud at the meeting. I wish Wik to be redressed. I know, too, that I have been silent too long, but one does not like to give up everything for a drunkard. Now it is another matter."

The women sat as if turned to stone. Anna Erikson, her voice trembling a little, said with a faint smile, –

"Now perhaps you will never care to come to see me again?"

"Oh, yes indeed! You were so young! It was nothing which you could help. – It was his fault for having such ideas."

She smiled. These were the hard beaks which would have torn her to pieces. The truth was not dangerous nor lying either. The young men were not waiting outside her door.

Did she know or did she not know that her eldest daughter had that very morning left her home and had gone to her father?

The sacrifice which Matts Wik had made to save his wife's honor became known. He was admired; he was derided. His letter was read aloud at the meeting. Some of those present wept with emotion. People came and pressed his hands on the street. His daughter moved to his house.

For several evenings after he was silent at the meetings. He felt no inspiration. At last they asked him to speak. He mounted the platform, folded his hands together and began.

When he had said a couple of words he stopped, confused. He did not recognize his own voice. Where was the lion's roar? Where the raging north wind? And where the torrent of words? He did not understand, could not understand.

He staggered back. "I cannot," he muttered. "God gives me no strength to speak yet." He sat down on a bench and buried his head in his hands. He gathered all his powers of thought to discover first what he wanted to talk about. Did he have to consider so in the old days? Could he consider now? His head whirled.

Perhaps it would go if he should stand up again, place himself where he was accustomed to stand, and begin with his usual prayer. He tried. His face turned ashy-grey. All glances were turned towards him. A cold sweat trickled down his forehead. He found not a word on his lips.

He sat down in his place and wept, moaning heavily. The gift was taken from him. He tried to speak, tried silently to himself. What should he talk about. His sorrow was taken from him. He had nothing to say to people which he was not allowed to tell them. He had no secret to disguise. He did not need to romance. Romance left him.

It was the agony of death; it was a struggle for life. He wished to hold fast that which was already gone. He wished to have his grief again in order to be able again to speak. His grief was gone; he could not get it back.

He staggered forward like a drunken man to the platform again and again: He stammered out a few meaningless words. He repeated like a lesson learned by heart what he had heard others say. He tried to imitate himself. He looked for devotion in the glances, for trembling silence, quickening breaths. He perceived nothing. That which had been his joy was taken from him.

He sank back into the darkness. He cursed, that he by his discourse had converted his wife and daughter. He had possessed the most precious of gifts and lost it. His pain was extreme. – But it is not by such grief that genius lives.

He was a painter without hands, a singer who had lost his voice. He had only spoken of his sorrow. What should he speak of now?

He prayed: "O God, when honor is dumb, and misjudgment speaks, give me back misjudgment! When happiness is dumb, but sorrow speaks, give me back sorrow!"

But the crown was taken from him. He sat there, more miserable than the most miserable, for he had been cast down from the heights of life. He was a fallen king.

A Christmas Guest

One of those who had lived the life of a pensioner at Ekeby was little Ruster, who could transpose music and play the flute. He was of low origin and poor, without home and without relations. Hard times came to him when the company of pensioners were dispersed.

He then had no horse nor cariole, no fur coat nor red-painted luncheon-basket. He had to go on foot from house to house and carry his belongings tied in a blue striped cotton handkerchief. He buttoned his coat all the way up to his chin, so that no one should need to know in what condition his shirt and waistcoat were, and in its deep pockets he kept his most precious possessions: his flute taken to pieces, his flat brandy bottle and his music-pen.

His profession was to copy music, and if it bad been as in the old days, there would have been no lack of work for him. But with every passing year music was less practiced in Värmland. The guitar, with its moldy, silken ribbon and its worn screws, and the dented horn, with faded tassels and cord were put away in the lumber-room in the attic, and the dust settled inches deep on the long, iron-bound violin boxes. Yet the less little Ruster had to do with flute and music-pen, so much the more must he turn to the brandy flask, and at last he became quite a drunkard. It was a great pity.

He was still received at the manor-houses as an old friend, but there were complaints when he came and joy when he went. There was an odor of dirt and brandy about him, and if he had only a couple of glasses of wine or one toddy, he grew confused and told unpleasant stories. He was the torment of the hospitable houses.

One Christmas he came to Löfdala, where Liljekrona, the great violinist, had his home. Liljekrona had also been one of the pensioners of Ekeby, but after the death of the major's wife, he returned to his quiet farm and remained there. Ruster came to him a few days before Christmas, in the midst of all the preparations, and asked for work. Liljekrona gave him a little copying to keep him busy.

"You ought to have let him go immediately," said his wife; "now he will certainly take so long with that that we will be obliged to keep him over Christmas."

"He must be somewhere," answered Liljekrona.

And he offered Ruster toddy and brandy, sat with him, and lived over again with him the whole Ekeby time. But he was out of spirits and disgusted by him, like everyone else, although he would not let it be seen, for old friendship and hospitality were sacred to him.

In Liljekrona's house for three weeks now they had been preparing to receive Christmas. They had been living in discomfort and bustle, had sat up with dip-lights and torches till their eyes grew red, had been frozen in the out-house with the salting of meat and in the brew-house with the brewing of the beer. But both the mistress and the servants gave themselves up to it all without grumbling.

When all the preparations were done and the holy evening come, a sweet enchantment would sink down over them. Christmas would loosen all tongues, so that jokes and jests, rhymes and merriment would flow of themselves without effort. Everyone's feet would wish to twirl in the dance, and from memory's dark corners words and melodies would rise, although no one could believe that they were there. And then everyone was so good, so good!

Now when Ruster came the whole household at Löfdala thought that Christmas was spoiled. The mistress and the older children and the old servants were all of the same opinion. Ruster caused them a suffocating disgust. They were moreover afraid that when he and Liljekrona began to rake up the old memories, the artist's blood would flame up in the great violinist and his home would lose him. Formerly he had not been able to remain long sit home.

No one can describe how they loved their master on the farm, since they had had him with them a couple of years. And what he had to give! How much he was to his home, especially at Christmas! He did not take his place on any sofa or rocking-stool, but on a high, narrow wooden bench in the corner of the fireplace. When he was settled there he started off on adventures. He traveled about the earth, climbed up to the stars, and even higher. He played and talked by turns, and the whole household gathered about him and listened. Life grew proud and beautiful when the richness of that one soul shone on it.

Therefore they loved him as they loved Christmas time, pleasure, the spring sun. And when little Ruster came, their Christmas peace was destroyed. They had worked in vain if he was coming to tempt away their master. It was unjust that the drunkard should sit at the Christmas table in a happy house and spoil the Christmas pleasure.

On the forenoon of Christmas Eve little Ruster had his music written out, and he said something about going, although of course he meant to stay.

Liljekrona had been influenced by the general feeling, and therefore said quite lukewarmly and indifferently that Ruster had better stay where he was over Christmas.

Little Ruster was inflammable and proud. He twirled his moustache and shook back the black artist's hair that stood like a dark cloud over his head. What did Liljekrona mean? Should he stay because he had nowhere else to go? Oh, only think how they stood and waited for him in the big ironworks in the parish of Bro! The guest-room was in order, the glass of welcome filled. He was in great haste. He only did not know to which he ought to go first.

"Very well," answered Liljekrona, "you may go if you will."

After dinner little Ruster borrowed horse and sleigh, coat and furs. The stable boy from Löfdala was to take him to some place in Bro and drive quickly back, for it threatened snow.

No one believed that he was expected, or that there was a single place in the neighborhood where he was welcome. But they were so anxious to be rid of him that they put the thought aside and let him depart. "He wished it himself," they said; and then they thought that now they would be glad.

But when they gathered in the dining room at five o'clock to drink tea and to dance round the Christmas tree, Liljekrona was silent and out of spirits. He did not seat himself on the bench; he touched neither tea nor punch; he could not remember any polka; the violin was out of order. Those who could play and dance had to do it without him.

Then his wife grew uneasy; the children were discontented, everything in the house went wrong. It was the most lamentable Christmas Eve.

The porridge turned sour; the candles sputtered; the wood smoked; the wind stirred up the snow and blew bitter cold into the rooms. The stable boy who had driven Ruster did not come home. The cook wept; the maids scolded.

Finally Liljekrona remembered that no sheaves had been put out for the sparrows, and he complained aloud of all the women about him who abandoned old customs and were new-fangled and heartless. They understood well enough that what tormented him was remorse that he had let little Ruster go away from his home on Christmas Eve.

After a while he went to his room, shut the door and began to play as he had not played since he had ceased roaming. It was full of hate and scorn, full of longing and revolt. You thought to bind me, but you must forge new fetters. You thought to make me as small-minded as yourselves, but I turn to larger things, to the open. Commonplace people, slaves of the home, hold me prisoner if it is in your power!

When his wife heard the music, she said: "Tomorrow he is gone, if God does not work a miracle in the night. Our inhospitableness has brought on just what we thought we could avoid."

In the meantime little Ruster drove about in the snowstorm. He went from one house to the other and asked if there was any work for him to do, but he was not received anywhere. They did not even ask him to get out of the sledge. Some had their houses full of guests, others were going away on Christmas Day. "Drive to the next neighbor," they all said.

He could come and spoil the pleasure of an ordinary day, but not of Christmas Eve. Christmas Eve came but once a year, and the children had been rejoicing in the thought of it all the autumn. They could not put that man at a table where there were children. Formerly they had been glad to see him, but not since he had become a drunkard. Where should they put the fellow, moreover? The servants' room was too plain and the guest-room too fine.

So little Ruster had to drive from house to house in the blinding snow. His wet moustache hung limply down over his mouth; his eyes were bloodshot and blurred, but the brandy was blown out of his brain. He began to wonder and to be amazed. Was it possible, was it possible that no one wished to receive him?

Then all at once he saw himself. He saw how miserable and degraded he was, and he understood that he was odious to people. "It is the end of me," he thought. "No more copying of music, no more flute-playing. No one on earth needs me; no one has compassion on me."

The storm whirled and played, tore apart the drifts and piled them up again, took a pillar of snow in its arms and danced out into the plain, lifted one flake up to the clouds and chased another down into a ditch. "It is so, it is so," said little Ruster; "while one dances and whirls it is play, but when one must be buried in the drift and forgotten, it is sorrow and grief." But down they all have to go, and now it was his turn. To think that he had now come to the end!

He no longer asked where the man was driving him; he thought that he was driving in the land of death.

Little Ruster made no offerings to the gods that night. He did not curse flute-playing or the life of a pensioner; he did not think that it had been better for him if he had plowed the earth or sewn shoes. But he mourned that he was now a worn-out instrument, which pleasure could no longer use. He complained of no one, for he knew that when the horn is cracked and the guitar will not stay in tune, they must go.

He became all at once a very humble man. He understood that it was the end of him, on this Christmas Eve. Hunger and cold would destroy him, for he understood nothing, was good for nothing and had no friends.

The sledge stops, and suddenly it is light about him, and he hears friendly voices, and there is someone who is helping him into a warm room, and someone who is pouring warm tea into him. His coat is pulled off him, and several people cry that he is welcome, and warm hands rub life into his benumbed fingers.

He was so confused by it all that he did not come to his senses for nearly a quarter of an hour. He could not possibly comprehend that he had come back to Löfdala. He had not been at all conscious that the stable boy had grown tired of driving about in the storm and had turned home.

Nor did he understand why he was now so well received in Liljekrona's house. He could not know that Liljekrona's wife understood what a weary journey he had made that Christmas Eve, when he had been turned away from every door where he had knocked. She felt such compassion on him that she forgot her own troubles.

Liljekrona went on with the wild playing up in his room; he did not know that Ruster had come. The latter sat meanwhile in the dining room with the wife and the children. The servants, who used also to be there on Christmas Eve, had moved out into the kitchen away from their mistress's trouble.

The mistress of the house lost no time in setting Ruster to work. "You hear, I suppose," she said, "that Liljekrona does nothing but play all the evening, and I must attend to setting the table and the food. The children are quite forsaken. You must look after these two smallest."

Children were the kind of people with whom little Ruster had had least intercourse. He had met them neither in the bachelor's wing nor in the campaign tent, neither in wayside inns nor on the highways. He was almost shy of them, and did not know what he ought to say that was fine enough for them.

He took out his flute and taught them how to finger the stops and holes. There was one of four years and one of six. They had a lesson on the flute and were deeply interested in it. "This is A," he said, "and this is C," and then he blew the notes. Then the young people wished to know what kind of an A and C it was that was to be played.

Ruster took out his score and made a few notes.

"No," they said, "that is not right." And they ran away for an A B C book.

Little Ruster began to hear their alphabet. They knew it and they did not know it. What they knew was not very much. Ruster grew eager; he lifted the little boys up, each on one of his knees, and began to teach them. Liljekrona's wife went out and in and listened quite in amazement. It sounded like a game, and the children were laughing the whole time, but they learned.

Ruster kept on for a while, but he was absent from what he was doing. He was turning over the old thoughts from out in the storm. It was good and pleasant, but nevertheless it was the end of him. He was worn out. He ought to be thrown away. And all of a sudden he put his hands before his face and began to weep.

Liljekrona's wife came quickly up to him.

"Ruster," she said, "I can understand that you think that all is over for you. You cannot make a living with your music, and you are destroying yourself with brandy. But it is not the end, Ruster."

"Yes," sobbed the little flute-player.

"Do you see that to sit as tonight with the children, that would be something for you? If you would teach children to read and write, you would be welcomed everywhere. That is no less important an instrument on which to play, Ruster, than flute and violin. Look at them, Ruster!"

She placed the two children in front of him, and he looked up, blinking as if he had looked at the sun. It seemed as if his little, blurred eyes could not meet those of the children, which were big, clear and innocent.

"Look at them, Ruster!" repeated Liljekrona's wife.

"I dare not," said Ruster, for it was like a purgatory to look through the beautiful child eyes to the unspotted beauty of their souls.

Liljekrona's wife laughed loud and joyously. "Then you must accustom yourself to them, Ruster. You can stay in my house as schoolmaster this year."

Liljekrona heard his wife laugh and came out of his room.

"What is it?" he said. "What is it?"

"Nothing," she answered, "but that Ruster has come again, and that I have engaged him as schoolmaster for our little boys."

Liljekrona was quite amazed. "Do you dare?" he said, "do you dare? Has he promised to give up—"

"No," said the wife; "Ruster has promised nothing. But there is much about which he must be careful when he has to look little children in the eyes every day. If it had not been Christmas, perhaps I would not have ventured; but when our Lord dared to place a little child who was his own son among us sinners, so can I also dare to let my little children try to save a human soul."

Liljekrona could not speak, but every feature and wrinkle in his face twitched and twisted as always when he heard anything noble.

Then he kissed his wife's hand as gently as a child who asks for forgiveness and cried aloud: "All the children must come and kiss their mother's hand."

They did so, and then they had a happy Christmas in Liljekrona's house.

Uncle Reuben

There was once, nearly eighty years ago, a little boy who went out into the marketplace to spin his top. The little boy's name was Reuben. He was not more than three years old, but he swung his little whip as bravely as anybody and made the top spin so that it was a pleasure to see it.

On that day, eighty years ago, it was beautiful spring weather. It was in the month of March, and the town was divided into two worlds; one white and warm, where the sun shone, and one cold and dark, where it was in shadow. The whole marketplace was in the sun except a narrow edge along one row of houses.

Now it happened that the little boy, brave as he was, grew tired of spinning his top and looked about for some place to rest. It was not hard to find. There were no benches or seats, but every house was supplied with stone steps. Little Reuben could not imagine anything better.

He was a conscientious little fellow. He had a vague feeling that his mother did not like to have him sit on strange people's steps. His mother was poor, but just on that account it must never look as if they wanted to take anything of anybody. So he went and sat on their own stone steps, for they also lived on the marketplace.

The steps lay in the shadow, and it was very cold there. The little fellow leaned his head against the railing, drew up his legs and made himself comfortable. For a little while he watched the sunlight dance out in the marketplace and the boys running and spinning tops – then he shut his eyes and went to sleep.

He must have slept an hour. When he awoke he did not feel so well as when he fell asleep; everything felt so dreadfully uncomfortable. He went in to his mother crying, and his mother saw that he was ill and put him to bed. And in a couple of days the boy was dead.

But that is not the end of his story. It happened that his mother mourned for him from the depths of her heart with a sorrow which defies years and death. His mother had several other children, many cares occupied her time and thoughts, but there was always a corner in her heart where her son Reuben dwelt undisturbed. He was ever alive to her. When she saw a group of children playing in the marketplace, he too was running there, and when she went about her house, she believed fully and firmly that the little boy was still sitting and sleeping out on those dangerous stone steps. Certainly none of her living children were so constantly in her thoughts as her dead one.

Some years after his death little Reuben had a sister, and when she grew to be old enough to run out on the marketplace and spin tops, it happened that she too sat down on the stone steps to rest. But her mother felt instantly as if someone had pulled her skirt. She came out and seized the little sister so roughly, when she lifted her up, that she remembered it as long as she lived.

And as little did she forget how strange her mother's face was and how her voice trembled, when she said: "Do you know that you once had a little brother, whose name was Reuben, and he died because he sat on these stone steps and caught cold? You do not want to die and leave your mother, Berta?"

Brother Reuben soon became just as living to his brothers and sisters as to his mother. She was able to make them see with her eyes and they too soon saw him sitting out on the stone steps. And it naturally never occurred to them to sit down there. Yes, whenever they saw anyone sitting on stone steps, or on a stone railing, or on a stone by the roadside, they felt a prick in their heart and thought of Brother Reuben.

Besides, Brother Reuben was always placed highest of all the children when they spoke of him among themselves. For they all knew that they were a troublesome and fatiguing family, who only gave their mother care and inconvenience. They could not believe that she would grieve much at losing any of them. But as she really mourned for Brother Reuben, it was certain that he must have been much better than they were.

They would often think: "Oh, if we could only give mother as much joy as Brother Reuben!" And yet no one knew anything more about him than that he had played top and caught cold on the stone steps. But he must have been something wonderful, as their mother had such a love for him.

He was wonderful too; he was more of a joy to his mother than any of the children. Her husband died and she worked in care and want. But the children had so strong a faith in their mother's grief for the little three-year-old boy, that they were convinced that if he had lived she would not have mourned over her misfortunes. And every time they saw their mother weep, they thought that it was because Brother Reuben was dead, or because they were not like Brother Reuben. Soon enough an ever-growing desire was born in them to rival their little dead brother in their mother's affection. There was nothing that they would not have done for her, if she had only cared as much for them as for him. And it was on account of that longing, I think, that Brother Reuben did more good than any of the other children.

Fancy that when the eldest brother had earned his first money by rowing a stranger over the river, he came and gave it to his mother without reserving a penny! Then his mother looked so happy that he swelled with pride, and could not help betraying how ambitious beyond measure he had been.

"Mother, am I not now as good as Brother Reuben?" His mother looked at him questioningly. She seemed as if she was comparing his fresh, glowing face with the little pale boy out on the stone steps. And she would have liked to have answered yes, if she had been able, but she could not.

"I am very fond of you, Ivan, but you will never be like Reuben."

It was beyond their powers; all the children realized it, and yet they could not help trying.

They grew up strong and capable; they worked their way up to wealth and consideration, while Brother Reuben only sat still on his stone steps. But he still had a start; he could not be overtaken.

And at every success, every improvement, as they by degrees were able to offer their mother a good home and comfort, it had to be reward enough for them for their mother to say: "Ah, if my little Reuben could have seen that!"

Brother Reuben followed his mother through the whole of her life, even to her deathbed. It was he who robbed the death pangs of their sting, since she knew that they bore her to him. In the midst of her greatest suffering the mother could smile at the thought that she was going to meet little Reuben.

And so died one whose faithful love had exalted and deified a poor little three-year-old boy.

But neither was that the end of little Reuben's story. To all the brothers and sisters he had become a symbol of their life of endeavor, of their love for their mother, of all the touching memories from the years of struggle and failure. There was always something rich and warm in their voices when they spoke of him.

So he also glided into the lives of the children of his brothers and sisters. His mother's love had raised him to greatness, and the great influence generation after generation.

Sister Berta had a son, who had much to do with Uncle Reuben.

He was four years old the day he sat on the curbstone and stared down into the gutter. It was full of rain water. Sticks and straws were carried past in wild swirlings down to the sea. The little boy sat and looked on with that pleasant calm that people feel in following the adventurous existence of others, when they themselves are in safety.

But his peaceful philosophizing was interrupted by his mother, who, the moment she saw him, thought of the stone steps at home and of her brother.

"Oh, my dear little boy," she said, "do not sit there! Do you know that your mamma had a little brother whose name was Reuben, and he was four years old just like you? He died because he sat on just such a curbstone and caught cold."

The little boy did not like being disturbed in his pleasant thoughts. He sat still and philosophized, while his yellow, curly hair fell down into his eyes.

Berta would not have done it for anyone else, but for her dear brother's sake she shook her little boy quite roughly. And so he learned respect for Uncle Reuben.

Another time this little yellow-haired man had fallen on the ice; he had been thrown down out of sheer spite by a big, naughty boy, and there he sat and cried to show how badly he had been treated, especially as his mother could not be very far off.

But he had forgotten that his mother was first and last Uncle Reuben's sister. When she caught sight of Axel sitting on the ice, she did not come with anything soothing or consoling, but only with that everlasting:

"Do not sit so, my little boy! Think of Uncle Reuben, who died when he was five years old, just as you are now, because he sat down in a snowdrift."

The boy stood up instantly when he heard her speak of Uncle Reuben, but he felt a chill in his very heart. How could mamma talk about Uncle Reuben when her little boy was in such distress! Axel had no objection to his sitting and dying wherever he pleased, but now it seemed as if he wished to take his own mamma away from him, and that Axel could not bear. So he learned to hate Uncle Reuben.

High up on the stairway in Axel's home was a stone railing, which was dizzily beautiful to sit on. Far below lay the stone floor of the hall, and he who sat astride up there could dream that he was being borne along over abysses. Axel called the balustrade the good steed Grane. On his back he bounded over burning ramparts into an enchanted castle. There he sat proud and bold with his long curls waving, and fought

Saint George's fight with the dragon. And as yet it had not occurred to Uncle Reuben to want to ride there.

But of course he came. Just as the dragon was writhing in the agony of death and Axel sat in lofty consciousness of victory, he heard his nurse call: "Little Axel, do not sit there! Think of Uncle Reuben, who died when he was eight years old, just as you are now, because he sat and rode on a stone railing. You must never sit there again."

Such a jealous old pudding-head, that Uncle Reuben! He could not bear it, of course, because Axel was killing dragons and rescuing princesses. If he did not look out, he, Axel, would show that he could win glory too. If he should jump down to that stone floor and dash his brains out, he would feel himself thrown into the shade, that big liar.

Poor Uncle Reuben! The poor, good little boy who went to play top out in the sunny marketplace! Now he was to learn what it was to be a great man.

It was in the country at Uncle Ivan's. A number of the cousins had gathered in the beautiful garden. Axel was there, filled with his hatred of his Uncle Reuben. He was longing to know if he was tormenting any other besides himself, but there was something which made him afraid to ask. It was as if he was going to commit some sacrilege.

At last the children were left to themselves. No big people were present. Then Axel asked if they had ever heard of Uncle Reuben.

He saw how all the eyes flashed and that many small fists were clenched, but it seemed as if the little mouths had been taught respect for Uncle Reuben. "Hush!" said the whole crowd.

"No!" said Axel; "I want to know if there is anyone else whom he tortures, for I think he is the most troublesome of all uncles."

That one brave word broke the dam which had held in the indignation of those tormented childhearts. There was a great murmuring and shouting. So must a crowd of nihilists look when they revile an autocrat.

The poor, great man's register of sins was unrolled. Uncle Reuben persecuted the children of all his brothers and sisters. Uncle Reuben died wherever he chose. Uncle Reuben was always the same age as the child whose peace he wished to disturb.

And they had to show respect to him, although he was quite plainly a liar. They might hate him in the most silent depths of their heart, but overlook him or show him disrespect, no, then they were stopped.

What an air the old people put on when they spoke of him! Had he ever really done anything so wonderful? To sit down and die was nothing so surprising. And whatever great thing he may have done, it was certain that he was now abusing his power. He opposed the children in everything that they wanted to do, the old scarecrow. He drove them from a noonday nap in the grass. He had discovered their best hiding places in the park and forbidden them to go there. His last performance was to ride on barebacked horses and to drive in the hay-rigging.

They were all sure that the poor thing had never been more than three years old. And now he fell upon the big children of fourteen and insisted that he was their age. It was the most provoking thing.

It was perfectly incredible what came to light about him. He had fished from the dam; he had rowed in the little flat-bottomed boat; he had climbed up in the willow which hangs over the water, and in which it was so nice to sit; yes, he had even slept on the powder-horn.

But they were all certain that there was no escape from his tyranny. It was a relief to have spoken out, but not a remedy. They could not rebel against Uncle Reuben.

You never would have believed it, but when these children grew to be big and had children of their own, they immediately began to make use of Uncle Reuben, just as their parents had done before them.

And their children again, the young people who are growing up now, have learned their lesson so well, that it happened one summer out in the country that a five-year-old boy came up to his old grandmother Berta, who had sat down on the steps while waiting for the carriage: –

"Grandmother once had a brother whose name was Reuben."

"You are quite right, my little boy," grandmother said, and stood up instantly.

That was as much of a sign to the young people as if they had seen an old Royalist bow before King Charles's portrait. It made them understand that Uncle Reuben always must remain great, however he abused his position, only because he had been so deeply loved.

In these days, when all greatness is so carefully examined, he has to be used with greater moderation than formerly. The limit for his age is lower; trees, boats and powder-horns 'are safe from him, but nothing of stone which can be sat upon can escape him.

And the children, the children of the day, treat him quite otherwise than their parents did. They criticize him openly and frankly. Their parents no longer understand how to inspire blind, terrified obedience. Little boarding-schoolgirls discuss Uncle Reuben and wonder if he is anything but a myth. A six-year-old child proposes that he should prove by experiment that it is impossible to catch a mortal cold on stone steps.

But that is only a passing mood. That generation in their heart of hearts is just as convinced of Uncle Reuben's greatness as the preceding one and obey him just as they did. The day will come when those scoffers will go down to the home of their ancestors, try to find the old stone steps, and raise on it a tablet with a golden inscription.

They joke about Uncle Reuben for a few years, but as soon as they are grown and have children to bring up, they will become convinced of the use and need of the great man.

"Oh, my little child, do not sit on those stone steps! Your mother's mother had an uncle whose name was Reuben. He died when he was your age, because he sat down to rest on just such steps."

So will it be as long as the world lasts.

Downie

I

I think I can see them as they drive away. Quite distinctly I can see his stiff, silk hat with its broad, curving brim, such as they had in the forties, his light waistcoat and his stock. I also see his handsome, clean-shaven face with its small, small whiskers, his high stiff collar, and the graceful dignity of his slightest movement. He is sitting on the right in the chaise and is just taking up the reins, and beside him is sitting that little woman. God bless her! I see her even more distinctly. Like a picture I have before me that narrow, little face, and the hat that frames it, tied under the chin, the dark-brown, smoothly combed hair, and the big shawl with the embroidered silk flowers. The chaise in which they are driving has a seat with a green, fluted back, and of course the innkeeper's horse which is to take them the first six miles is a little fat sorrel.

I lost my heart to her from the very first moment. There is no sense in it, for she is the most insignificant little person; but I was won by seeing all the eyes that followed her when she drove away. In the first place, I see how her father and mother look after her from where they stand in the doorway of the baker's shop. Her father even has tears in his eyes, but her mother has no time to weep yet. She must use her eyes to look at her daughter as long as the latter can wave and nod to her. And then of course there are merry greetings from the children in the little street and roguish glances from all the pretty, little factory girls from behind windows and doors, and dreamy looks from some of the young salesmen and apprentices. But all nod good-will and god-speed to her. And then there are anxious glances from some poor, old women, who come out and curtsey and take off their spectacles to be able to see her as she drives by in state. But I cannot see a single unfriendly look following her; no, not in the whole length of the street.

When she is out of sight, her father wipes the tears from his eyes with his sleeve.

"Don't be sad now, mother!" he says. "You will see that she will come out all right. Downie will manage, mother, even if she is so little."

"Father," says the mother with great emphasis, "you speak in a strange way. Why should Anne-Marie not be able to manage it? She is as good as anybody."

"Of course she is, mother; but still, mother, still – I would not be in her shoes, nor go where she is going. No, that I would not!"

"Well, and what good would that do, you ugly old baker!" says mother, who sees that he is so uneasy about the girl that he needs to be cheered with a little joke. And father laughs, for he does that as easily as he cries. And then the old people go back into their shop.

In the meantime Downie, the little silken flower, is in very good spirits as she drives along the road. A little afraid of her betrothed, perhaps; but in her heart Downie is a little afraid of everybody, and that is a great help to her, for on account of it everyone tries to show her that they are not dangerous.

Never has she had such respect for Maurits as today. Now that they have left the back street, and all her friends are behind them, it seems to her that Maurits really grows to something big. His hat and collar and whiskers stiffen, and the bow of his necktie swells. His voice grows thick in his throat, and he speaks with difficulty. She feels a little depressed by it, but it is splendid to see Maurits so impressive.

Maurits is so clever; he has so much advice to give! – it is hard to believe – but Maurits talks only sense the whole way. But that is just like Maurits. He asks her if she understands clearly what this journey means to him. Does she think it is only a pleasure trip along the country road? Thirty miles in a good chaise with her betrothed by her side did seem quite like a pleasure trip, and a beautiful place to drive to, a rich uncle to visit – perhaps she has thought that it was only for amusement?

Fancy if he knew that she had prepared herself for this journey by a long conference with her mother before they went to bed; and by a long succession of anxious dreams through the night, and with prayers, and with tears! But she pretends to be stupid, in order to get more enjoyment out of Maurits's wisdom. He likes to show it, and she is glad to let him.

"The real trouble is that you are so sweet," says Maurits; for that was how he had come to care for her, and it was really very stupid of him. His father was not at all in favor of it. And his mother! He hardly dared to think of what a fuss she had made when Maurits had informed her that he had engaged himself to a poor girl from a back street – a girl who had no education, no accomplishments, and who was not even pretty; only sweet.

In Maurits's eyes, of course, the daughter of a baker was just as good as the son of a burgomaster, but everyone did not have such liberal views as he. If Maurits had not had his rich uncle, it could never have come to anything; for he was only a student, and had nothing to marry on. But if they now could win his uncle over their way was clear.

I see them so plainly as they drive along the road. She looks a little unhappy as she listens to his wisdom. But she is content in her thoughts! How sensible Maurits is! And when he speaks of the sacrifices he is making for her, it is only his way of saying how much he cares for her.

And if she had expected that alone together on such a beautiful day he perhaps might be not quite the same as when they sat at home with her mother – but that would not have been right of Maurits. She is proud of him.

He is telling her what kind of a man his uncle is. If he will befriend them their fortune is made. Uncle Theodore is incredibly rich. He owns eleven smelting-furnaces, and farms and houses besides, and mines and stocks. To all these Maurits is the proper heir. But Uncle Theodore is a little uncertain to have to do with when it concerns anyone he does not like. If he is not pleased with Maurits's wife, he can will away everything.

The little face grows paler and smaller, but Maurits only stiffens and swells. There is not much chance of Anne-Marie's turning his uncle's head as she did his. His uncle is quite a different kind of man. His taste – well, Maurits does not think much of his taste - but he thinks that it would be something loud-voiced, something flashing and red which would strike Uncle. Besides, he is a confirmed old bachelor – thinks women are only a bother. The most important thing is that he shall not dislike her too much. Maurits will take care of the rest. But she must not be silly. Is she crying – ! Oh, if she does not look better by the time they arrive, Uncle will send them off inside of a minute. She is glad for their sakes that Uncle is not as clever as Maurits. She hopes it is no sin against Maurits to think that it is good that Uncle is quite a different sort of person. For fancy, if Maurits had been Uncle, and two poor young people had come driving to him to get aid in life; then Maurits, who is so sensible, would certainly have begged them to return whence they came, and wait to get married until they had something to marry on.

Uncle, however, was decidedly terrifying in his own way. He drank, and gave great parties, where everybody was very lively, and he did not at all understand how to manage his affairs. He must know that everyone cheated him, but he was nonetheless cheerful. And heedless! – the burgomaster had sent by Maurits some shares in an undertaking that was not prosperous; but Uncle would buy them of him, Maurits had said. Uncle did not care where he threw his money away. He had stood in town in the marketplace and tossed silver to the street boys. Playing away a couple of thousand crowns in a single night, or lighting his pipe with ten-crown notes, were among the things Uncle did.

Thus they drove on, and thus they talked while they were driving.

They arrived toward evening. Uncle's "residence," as he called it, did not stand by the ironworks. It lay far from all smoke and hammering, on the slope of the mountain, looking over a wide view of lakes and long hills. It was a stately building, with wooded lawns and groves of birches round about it, but few cultivated fields, for the place was a pleasure palace, not a farm.

The young people drove up an avenue lined with birches and elms. Then they drove between two low, thick rows of hedges and were about to turn up to the house.

But just where the road turned, a triumphal arch was raised, and there stood Uncle with his dependents to greet them. Downie never could have believed that Maurits would have prepared such a reception for her. Her heart grew light, and she seized his hand and pressed it in gratitude. More she could not do then, for they were just under the arch.

And there he stood, the well-known man, the ironmaster, Theodore Fristeat, big and black-bearded, and beaming with good-will. He waved his hat and shouted hurrah, and all the people shouted hurrah, and tears rose in Anne-Marie's eyes, although she was smiling. And of course they all had to like her from the very first moment, if only for her way of looking at Maurits. For she thought that they were all there for his sake, and she had to turn her eyes away from the whole spectacle to look at him, as he took off his hat with a sweep and bowed so beautifully and royally. Oh, such a look as she gave him! Uncle Theodore almost left off hurrahing and felt like swearing when he saw it.

No, she wished no harm to anyone on earth, but if the estate really had been Maurits's, it would have been very suitable. It was most impressive to see him, as he stood on the steps of the porch and turned to the people to thank them. The ironmaster was stately too, but what was his manner compared to Maurits's. He only helped her down from the carriage, and took her shawl and hat like a footman, while Maurits lifted his hat from his white brow and said: "Thank you, my children!" No, the ironmaster certainly had no manners; for as he profited by his rights as an uncle and took her in his arms, he noticed that she managed to look at Maurits while he was kissing her, and he swore, really swore quite fiercely. Downie was not accustomed to find anyone disagreeable, but it certainly would be no easy task to please Uncle Theodore.

"Tomorrow," says uncle, "there will be a big dinner here, and a ball, but today you young people must rest after your journey. Now we will eat our supper, and then we will go to bed."

They are escorted into a drawing room, and there they are left alone. The ironmaster rushes out like a wind which is afraid of being shut in. Five minutes later he is rolling down the avenue in his big carriage, and the coachman is driving so that the horses seem to be lying along the ground. After another five minutes uncle is there again, and now an old lady is sitting beside him in the carriage.

And in he comes, with a kind, talkative old lady on his arm. And she takes Anne-Marie and embraces her, but Maurits she greets more stiffly. No one can take any liberties with Maurits.

However, Anne-Marie is very glad that this pleasant old lady has come. She and the ironmaster have such a merry way of joking with one another.

But when they have said good-night and Anne-Marie has come into her little room, something too tiresome and provoking happens.

Uncle and Maurits are walking in the garden, and she knows that Maurits is unfolding his plans for the future. Uncle does not seem to be saying anything at all; he is only walking and striking the blades of grass with his stick. But Maurits will persuade him fast enough that the best thing for him to do is to give Maurits a position as manager of one of his steel-works, if he does not care to give him the works outright. Maurits has grown so practical since he has been in love. He often says: "Is it not best for me, who am to be a great landowner, to make myself familiar with it all? What is the use of taking my bar examinations?"

They are walking directly under the window and nothing prevents them from seeing that she is sitting there; but as they do not mind it, no one can ask that she shall not hear what they are saying. It is really just as much her affair as it is Maurits's.

Then Uncle Theodore suddenly stops and he looks angry. He looks quite furious, she thinks, and she almost calls to Maurits to take care. But it is too late, for Uncle Theodore has seized Maurits, crushed his ruffle, and is shaking him till he twists like an eel. Then he slings him from him with such force that Maurits staggers backwards any! would have fallen if he had not found support in a tree trunk. And there Maurits stands and gasps "What?" Yes, what else should he say?

Ah, never has she admired Maurits's self-control so much! He does not throw himself upon Uncle Theodore and fight him. He only looks calmly superior, merely innocently surprised. She understands that he controls himself so that the journey may not be for nothing. He is thinking of her, and is controlling himself.

Poor Maurits! it seems that his uncle is angry with him on her account. He asks if Maurits does not know that his uncle is a bachelor when he brings his betrothed here without bringing her mother with him. Her mother! Downie is offended in Maurits's behalf. It was her mother who had excused herself and said that she could not leave the bakery. Maurits answers so too, but his uncle will accept no excuses. – Well, his mother, then; she could have done her son that service. Yes, if she had been too haughty they had better have stayed where they were. What would they have done if his old lady had not been able to come? And how could a betrothed couple travel alone through the country? – Really, Maurits was not dangerous. No, that he had never believed, but people's tongues are dangerous. – Well, and finally it was that chaise! Had Maurits ferreted out the most ridiculous vehicle in the whole town? To let that child shake thirty miles in a chaise, and to let him raise a triumphal arch for a chaise! – He would like to shake him again! To let his uncle shout hurrah for a tip-cart! He was getting too unreasonable. How she admired Maurits for being so calm! She would like to join in the game and defend Maurits, but she does not believe that he would like it.

And before she goes to sleep, she lies and thinks out everything she would have said to defend Maurits. Then she falls asleep and starts up again, and in her ears rings an old saying: –

"A dog stood on a mountaintop,
He barked aloud and would not stop.
His name was you, His name was I,
His name was all in Earth and Sky.
What was his name?
His name was why."

The saying had irritated her many a time. Oh, how stupid she had thought the dog was! But now half asleep, she confuses the dog "What" with Maurits and she thinks that the dog has his white forehead. Then she laughs. She laughs as easily as she cries. She has inherited that from her father.

II

How has "it" come? That which she dares not call by name?

"It" has come like the dew to the grass, like the color to the rose, like the sweetness to the berry, imperceptibly and gently without announcing itself beforehand.

It is also no matter how "it" came or what "it" is. Were it good or evil, fair or foul, still it is forbidden; that which never ought to exist. "It" makes her anxious, sinful, unhappy.

"It" is that of which she never wishes to think. "It" is what shall be torn away and thrown out; and yet it is nothing that can be seized and caught. She shuts her heart to "it," but it comes in just the same. "It" turns back the blood in her veins and flows there, drives the thoughts from her brain and reigns there, dances through her nerves and trembles in her fingertips. It is everywhere in her, so that if she had been able to take away everything else of which her body consisted and to have left "it" behind, there would remain a complete impression of her. And yet "it" was nothing.

She wishes never to think of "it," and yet she has to think of "it" constantly. How has she become so wicked? And then she searches and wonders how "it" came.

Ah Downie! How tender are our souls, and how easily awakened are our hearts!

She was sure that "it" had not come at breakfast, surely not at breakfast.

Then she had only been frightened and shy. She had been so terrified when she came down to breakfast and found no Maurits, only Uncle Theodore and the old lady.

It had been a clever idea of Maurits to go hunting; although it was impossible to discover what he was hunting in midsummer, as the old lady remarked. But he knew of course that it was wise to keep away from his uncle for a few hours until the latter became calm again. He could not know that she was so shy, nor that she had almost fainted when she had found him gone and herself left alone with uncle and the old lady. Maurits had never been shy. He did not know what torture it is.

That breakfast, that breakfast! Uncle had as a beginning asked the old lady if she had heard the story of Sigrid the beautiful. He did not ask Downie, neither would she have been able to answer. The old lady knew the story well, but he told it just the same. Then Anne-Marie remembered that Maurits had laughed at his uncle because in all his house he only had two books, and those were Afzelius' "Fairy Tales" and Nösselt's "Popular Stories for Ladies." "But those he knows," Maurits had said.

Anne-Marie had found the story pretty. She liked it when Bengt Lagman had pearls sewn on the breadth of homespun. She saw Maurits before her; how royally proud he would have looked when ordering the pearls! That was just the sort of thing Maurits would have done well.

But when uncle had come to that part of the story where Bengt Lagman went into the woods to avoid the meeting with his angry brother, and instead let his young wife meet the storm, then it became so plain that uncle understood Maurits had gone hunting to escape his wrath and that he knew how she thought to win him over. – Yes, yesterday, then they had been able to make plans, Maurits and she, how she should coquet with uncle, but today she had no thought of carrying them out. Oh, she had never behaved so foolishly! Every drop of blood streamed into her face, and her knife and fork fell with a terrible clatter out of her hands down on her plate.

But Uncle Theodore had shown no mercy and had gone on with the story until he came to that princely speech: "Had my brother not done it, I would have done it myself." He said it with such a strange emphasis that she was forced to look up and to meet his laughing brown eyes.

And when he saw the trouble staring from her eyes, he began to laugh like a boy. "What do you think," he cried, "Bengt Lagman thought when he came home and heard that 'Had my brother?' I think he stopped at home the next time."

Tears rose to Downie's eyes, and when Uncle saw that he laughed louder. "Yes, it is a fine partisan my nephew has chosen," he seemed to say, "You are not playing your part, my little girl." And every time she had looked at him the brown eyes had repeated: "Had my brother not done it, I would have done it myself." Downie was not quite sure that the eyes did not say "nephew." And fancy how she behaved. She began to cry, and rushed from the room.

But it was not then that "it" came, nor during the walk of the forenoon.

Then she was occupied with something quite different. Then she was overcome with pleasure at the beautiful place and that nature was so wonderfully near. She felt as if she had found again something she had lost long, long ago.

People thought she was a city girl. But she had become a country lass as soon as she put her foot on the sandy path. She felt instantly that she belonged to the country.

As soon as she had calmed down a little she had ventured out by herself to inspect the place. She had looked about her on the lawn in front of the door. Then she suddenly began to whirl about; she hung her hat on her arm and threw her shawl away. She drew the air into her lungs so that her nostrils were drawn together and whistled.

Oh, how brave she felt!

She made a few attempts to go quietly and sedately down to the garden, but that was not what attracted her. Turning off to one side, she started towards the big groups of barns and out-houses. She met a farm-girl and said a few words to her. She was surprised to hear how brisk her own voice sounded; it was like an officer at the front. And she felt how smart she looked when, with head proudly raised and a little on one side, moving with a quick, free motion and with a little switch in her hand, she entered the barn.

It was not, however, what she had expected. No long rows of horned creatures were there to impress her, for they were all out at pasture. A single calf stood in its pen and seemed to expect her to do something for him. She went up to him, raised herself on tiptoe, held her dress together with one hand and touched the calf's forehead with the finger-tips of the other.

As the calf still did not seem to think that she had done enough and stretched out his long tongue, she graciously let him lick her little finger. She could not resist looking about her, as if to find someone to admire her bravery. And she discovered that Uncle Theodore stood at the barn-door and laughed at her.

Then he had gone with her on her walk. But "it" did not come then, not then at all. It had only wonderfully come to pass that she was no longer afraid of Uncle Theodore. He was like her mother; he seemed to know all her faults and weaknesses, and it was so comfortable. She did not need to show herself better than she was.

Uncle Theodore wished to take her to the garden and to the terraces by the pond, but that was not to her mind. She wished to know what there could be in all those big buildings.

So he went patiently with her to the dairy and to the ice-house; to the wine-cellar and to the potato bins. He took the things in order, and showed her the larder, and the wood shed, and the carriage-house, and the laundry. Then he led her through the stable of the draught-horses, and that of the carriage horses; let her see the harness-room and the servants' rooms; the laborers' cottages and the wood-carving room. She became a little confused by all the different rooms that Uncle Theodore had considered necessary to establish on his estate; but her heart was glowing with enthusiasm at the thought of how splendid it must be to have all that to rule over. So she was not tired, although they walked through the sheep-houses and the piggeries, and looked in at the hens and the rabbits. She faithfully examined the weaving-rooms and the dairies, the smoke-house and the smithy, all with growing enthusiasm. Then they visited the big lofts; drying-rooms for the clothes and drying-rooms for the wood; hay-lofts, and lofts for dried leaves for the sheep to eat.

The dormant housewife in her awoke to life and consciousness at all this perfection. But most of all, she was moved by the great brewhouse and the two neat bakeries with the wide oven and the big table.

"Mother ought to see that," she said.

In the bakehouse they had sat down and rested, and she had told of her home. He was already like a friend, although his brown eyes laughed at everything she said.

At home everything was so quiet; no life, no variety. She had been a delicate child, and her parents had watched over her on account of it, and let her do nothing. It was only as play that she was allowed to help in the baking and in the shop. Somehow she came to tell him that her father called her Downie. She had also said: "Everybody spoils me at home except Maurits, and that is why I like him so much. He is so sensible with me! He never calls me Downie; only Anne-Marie. Maurits is so admirable."

Oh, how it had danced and laughed in uncle's eyes! She could have struck him with her switch. She repeated almost with a sob: "Maurits is so admirable."

"Yes, I know, I know," Uncle had answered. "He is going to be my heir." Whereupon she had cried: "Ah; Uncle Theodore, why do you not marry? Think how happy anyone would be to be mistress of such an estate!"

"How would it be then with Maurits's inheritance?" uncle had asked quite softly.

Then she had been silent for a long while, for she could not say to Uncle that she and Maurits did not ask for the inheritance, for that was just what they did do. She wondered if it was very ugly for them to do so. She suddenly had a feeling as if she ought to beg Uncle for forgiveness for some great wrong that they had done him. But she could not do that either.

When they came in again, Uncle's dog came to meet them. It was a tiny, little thing on the thinnest legs, with fluttering ears and gazellelike eyes; a nothing with a shrill, little voice.

"You wonder, perhaps, that I have such a little dog," Uncle Theodore had said.

"I suppose I do," she had answered.

"But, you see, it is not I who have chosen Jenny for my dog, but Jenny who has taken me as a master. You would like to hear the story, Downie?" That name he had instantly seized upon.

Yes, she would like it, although she understood that it would be something irritating he would say.

"Well, you see, when Jenny came here the first time she lay on the knees of a fine lady from the town, and had a blanket on her back and a cloth about her head. Hush, Jenny; it is true that you had it! And I thought what a little rat it was. But do you know when that little creature was put down on the ground here some memories of her childhood or something must have wakened in her. She scratched, and kicked, and tried to rub off her blanket. And then she behaved like the big dogs here; so we said that Jenny must have grown up in the country.

"She lay out on the doorstep and never even looked at the parlor sofa, and she chased the chickens, and stole the cat's milk, and barked at beggars, and darted about the horses' legs when we had guests. It was a pleasure and a joy to us to see how she behaved. You must understand, a little thing that had only lain in a basket and been carried on the arm! It was wonderful. And so when they were going to leave, Jenny would not go. She stood on the steps and whined so pitifully and jumped up on me, and really asked to be allowed to stay. So there was nothing for us to do but to let her stay. We were touched by the little creature; it was so small, and yet wished to be a country dog. But I had never thought that I should ever keep a lap dog. Soon, perhaps, I shall get a wife too."

Oh, how hard it is to be shy, to be uneducated! She wondered if Uncle had been very surprised when she rushed away so hurriedly. But she had felt as if he had meant her when he spoke of Jenny. And perhaps he had not at all. But any way – yes she had been so embarrassed. She could not have stayed.

But it was not then "it" came, not then.

Perhaps it was in the evening at the ball. Never had she had such a good time at any ball! But if anyone had asked her if she had danced much, she would have needed to reconsider and acknowledge that she had not. But it was the best proof that she had really enjoyed herself when she had not even noticed that she had been a little neglected.

She had so much enjoyed looking at Maurits. Just because she had been a little bit severe to him at breakfast and laughed at him yesterday, it was such a pleasure to her to see him at the ball. He had never seemed to her so handsome and so superior.

He had seemed to feel that she would consider herself injured because he had not talked and danced only with her. But it had been pleasure enough for her to see how everyone liked Maurits. As if she had wished to exhibit their love to the general gaze! Oh, Downie was not so foolish!

Maurits danced many dances with the beautiful Elizabeth Westling. But that had not troubled her at all, for Maurits had time after time come up and whispered: "You see, I can't get away from her. We are old friends. Here in the country they are so unaccustomed to have a partner who has been in society and can both dance and talk. You must lend me to the daughters of the county magnates for this evening, Anne-Marie."

But Uncle, too, gave way to Maurits. "Be host for this evening," he said to him, and Maurits was. He was everywhere. He led the dance, he led the drinking, and he made a speech for the county and for the ladies. He was wonderful. Both Uncle and she had watched Maurits, and then their eyes had met. Uncle had smiled and nodded to her. Uncle certainly was proud of Maurits. She had felt badly that Uncle did not really do justice to his nephew. Towards morning Uncle had been loud and quarrelsome. He had wanted to join the dance, but the girls drew back from him when he came up to them and pretended to be engaged.

"Dance with Anne-Marie," Maurits had said to his uncle, and it had sounded rather patronizing. She was so frightened that she quite shrank together.

Uncle was offended too, turned on his heel and went into the smoking-room.

Maurits came up to her and said with a hard, hard voice: –

"You are ruining everything, Anne-Marie. Must you look like that when Uncle wishes to dance with you? If you could know what he said to me yesterday about you! You must do something too, Anne-Marie. Do you think it is right to leave everything to me?"

"What do you wish me to do, Maurits?"

"Oh, now there is nothing; now the game is spoiled. Think all I had won this evening! But it is lost now."

"I will gladly ask Uncle's pardon, if you like, Maurits." And she really meant it. She was honestly sorry to have hurt Uncle.

"That is of course the only right thing to do; but one can ask nothing of anyone as ridiculously shy as you are."

She had not answered, but had gone straight to the smoking-room, which was almost empty. Uncle had thrown himself down in an arm-chair.

"Why will you not dance with me?" she had asked.

Uncle Theodore's eyes were closed. He opened them and looked long at her. It was a look full of pain that she met. It made her understand how a prisoner must feel when he thinks of his chains. It made her sorry for Uncle. It seemed as if he had needed her much more than Maurits, for Maurits needed no one. He was very well as he was. So she laid her hand on Uncle Theodore's arm quite gently and caressingly.

Instantly new life awoke in his eyes. He began to stroke her hair with his big hand. "Little mother," he had said.

Then "it" came over her while he stroked her hair. It came stealing, it came creeping, it came rushing, as when elves pass through dark woods.

III

One evening thin, soft clouds are floating in the sky; one evening all is still and mild; one evening the air is filled with fine white down from the aspens and poplars.

It is quite late, and no one is up except Uncle Theodore, who is walking in the garden and is considering how he can separate the young man and the young woman.

For never, never in the world shall it come to pass that Maurits leaves his house with her at his side while Uncle Theodore stands on the steps and wishes them a pleasant journey.

Is it a possibility to let her go at all, since she has filled the house for three days with merry chirping, since she in her quiet way has accustomed them to be cared for and petted by her, since they have all grown used to seeing that soft, supple little creature roving about everywhere. Uncle Theodore says to himself that it is not possible. He cannot live without her.

Just then he strikes against a dandelion which has gone to seed, and, like men's resolutions and men's promises, the white ball of down is scattered, its white floss flies out and is dispersed.

The night is not cold as the nights generally are in that part of the country. The warmth is kept in by the grey cloud blanket. The winds show themselves merciful for once and do not blow.

Uncle Theodore sees her, Downie. She is weeping because Maurits has forsaken her. But he draws her to him and kisses away her tears.

Soft and fine, the white down falls from the great ripe clusters of the trees, – so light that the air will scarcely let them fall, so fine and delicate that they hardly show on the ground.

Uncle Theodore laughs to himself when he thinks of Maurits. In thought he goes in to him the next morning while he is still lying in his bed. "Listen, Maurits," he means to say to him. "I do not wish to inspire you with false hopes. If you marry this girl, you need not expect a penny from me. I will not help to ruin your future."

"Do you think so badly of her, uncle?" Maurits will say.

"No, on the contrary; she is a nice girl, but still not the one for you. You shall have a woman like Elizabeth Westling. Be sensible, Maurits; what will become of you if you break off your studies and go into trade for that child's sake. You are not suited to it, my boy. Something more is needed for such work than to be able to lift your hat gracefully from your head and to say: 'Thank you, my children!' You are cut out and made for a civil official. You can become minister."

"If you have such a good opinion of me," Maurits will answer, "help me with my examination and let us afterwards be married!"

"Not at all, not at all. What do you think would become of your career if you had such a weight as a wife? The horse which drags the bread wagon does not go fast ahead. Think of the girl from the bakery as a minister's wife! No, you ought not to engage yourself for at least ten years, not before you have made your place. What would the result be if I helped you to be married? Every year you would come to me and beg for money. You and I would both weary of that."

"But, uncle, I am a man of honor. I have engaged myself."

"Listen, Maurits! Which is better? For her to go and wait for you for ten years, and then find that you will not marry her, or for you to break it off now? No, be decided, get up, take the chaise and go home before she wakes. It will never do at any rate for a betrothed couple to wander about the country by themselves. I will take care of the girl if you only give up this madness. My old friend will go home with her. You shall be supported by me so that you do not need to worry about your future. Now be sensible; you will please your parents by obeying me. Go now, without seeing her! I will talk to her. She will not stand in the way of your happiness. Do not try to see her before you leave, then you could grow soft-hearted, for she is sweet."

And at those words Maurits makes an heroic decision and goes his way.

And when he has gone, what will happen then?

"Scoundrel," sounds in the garden, loud and threateningly, as if to a thief. Uncle Theodore looks about him. Is it no one else? Is it only he calling so at himself?

What will happen afterwards? Oh, he will prepare her for Maurits's departure; show her that Maurits was not worthy of her; make her despise him. And then when she has cried her heart out on his breast, he shall so carefully, so skillfully make her understand what he feels, lure her, win her.

The down still falls. Uncle Theodore stretches out his big hand and catches a bit of it.

So fine, so light, so delicate! He stands and looks at it.

It falls about him, flake after flake. What will become of them? They will be driven by the wind, soiled by the earth, trampled upon by heavy feet.

He begins to feel as if that light down fell upon him with the heaviest weight. Who will be the wind; who will be the earth; who will be the shoe when it is a question of such defenseless little things?

And as a result of his extraordinary knowledge of Nösselt's "Popular Stories," an episode from one of them occurred to him like what he had just been thinking.

It was an early morning, not falling night as now. It was a rocky shore, and down by the sea sat a beautiful youth with a panther skin over his shoulder, with vine leaves in his hair, with thyrsus in his hand. Who was he? Oh, the god Bacchus himself.

And the rocky shore was Naxos. It was the seas of Greece the god saw. The ship with the black sails swiftly sailing towards the horizon was steered by Theseus and in the grotto, the entrance of which opened high up in a projection of the steep cliff, slept Ariadne.

During the night the young god had thought: "Is this mortal youth worthy of that divine girl!" And to test Theseus he had in a dream frightened him with the loss of his life, if he did not instantly forsake Ariadne. Then the latter had risen up, hastened to the ship, and fled away over the waves without even waking the girl to say good-bye.

Now the god Bacchus sat there smiling, rocked by the tenderest hopes, and waited for Ariadne.

The sun rose, the morning breeze freshened. He abandoned himself to smiling dreams. He would know well how to console the forsaken one; he, the god Bacchus himself.

Then she came. She walked out of the grotto with a beaming smile. Her eyes sought Theseus, they wandered farther away to the anchoring-place of the ship, to the sea – to the black sails.

And then with a piercing scream, without consideration, without hesitation, down into the waves, down to death and oblivion.

And there sat the god Bacchus, the consoler.

So it was. Thus had it actually happened. Uncle Theodore remembers that Nösselt adds in a few words that sympathetic poets affirm that Ariadne let herself be consoled by Bacchus. But the sympathizers were certainly wrong. Ariadne would not be consoled.

Good God, because she is good and sweet, so that he must love her, shall she for that reason be made unhappy!

As a reward for the sweet little smiles she had given him; because her soft little hand had lain so trustingly in his; because she had not been angry when he jested, shall she lose her betrothed and be made unhappy?

For which of all her misdemeanors shall she be condemned? Because she has shown him a room in his innermost soul, which seems to have stood fine and clean and unoccupied all these years awaiting just such a tender and motherly little woman; or because she has already such power over him that he hardly dares to swear lest she hear it; or for what shall she be condemned?

Oh, poor Bacchus, poor Uncle Theodore! It is not easy to have to do with such delicate, light bits of down. – They leap into the sea when they see the black sails.

Uncle Theodore swears softly because Downie has not black hair, red cheeks, coarse limbs.

Then another flake falls and it begins to speak: "It is I who would have followed you all your days. I would have whispered a warning in your ear at the card-table. I would have moved away the wineglass. You would have borne it from me." "I would," he whispers, "I would."

Another comes and speaks too: "It is I who would have reigned over your big house and made it cheery and warm. It is I who would have followed you through the desert of old age. I would have lighted your fire, have been your eyes and your staff. Should I have been fit for that?" "Sweet little Downie," he answers, "you would."

Again a flake comes and says: "I am so to be pitied. Tomorrow my betrothed is leaving me without even saying farewell. Tomorrow I shall weep, weep all day long, for I shall feel the shame of not being good enough for Maurits. And when I come home – I do not know how I shall be able to come home; how I can cross my father's threshold after this. The whole street will be full of whispering and gossip when I show myself. Everyone will wonder what evil thing I have done, to be so badly treated. Is it my fault that you love me?" He answers with a sob in his throat: "Do not speak so, little Downie! It is too soon to speak so."

He wanders there the whole night and towards midnight comes a little darkness. He is in great trouble; the heavy, sultry air seems to be still in terror of some crime which is to be committed in the morning.

He tries to calm the night by saying aloud: "I shall not do it."

Then the most wonderful thing happens. The night is seized with a trembling dread. It is no longer the little flakes which are falling, but round about him rustle great and small wings. He hears something flying but does not know whither.

They rush by him; they graze his cheek; they touch his clothes and hands; and he understands what it is. The leaves are falling from the trees; the flowers flee from their stalks; the wings fly away from the butterflies; the song forsakes the birds.

And he understands that when the sun rises his garden will be a waste. Empty, cold, and silent winter shall reign there; no play of butterflies; no song of birds.

He remains until the light comes again, and he is almost astonished when he sees the thick masses of leaves on the trees. "What is it, then," he says, "which is laid waste if it was not the garden? Not even a blade of grass is missing. It is I who must live in winter and cold hereafter, not the garden. It is as if the mainspring of life were gone. Ah, you old fool, this will pass like everything else. It is too much ado about a little girl."

IV

How very improperly "it" behaved the morning they were to leave! During the two days after the ball "it" had been rather something inspiring, something exciting; but now when Downie is to leave, when "it" realizes that the end has come, that "it" will never play any part in her life, then it changes to a death thrust, to a deathly coldness.

She feels as if she were dragging a body of stone down the stairs to the breakfast-room. She stretches out a heavy, cold hand of stone when she says good-morning; she speaks with a slow tongue of stone; smiles with hard stone lips. It is a labor, a labor.

But who can help being glad when everything is arranged according to old-fashioned faith and honor.

Uncle Theodore turns to Downie at breakfast and explains with a strangely harsh voice that he has decided to give Maurits the position of manager at Laxohyttan; but as the aforesaid young man, continued Uncle, with a strained attempt to return to his usual manner, is not much at home in practical occupations, he may not enter upon the position until he has a wife at his side. Has she, Miss Downie, tended her myrtle so well that she can have a crown and wreath in September?

She feels how he is looking into her face. She knows that he wishes to have a glance as thanks, but she does not look up.

Maurits leaps up. He embraces Uncle and makes a great deal of noise. "But, Anne-Marie, why do you not thank Uncle? You must kiss Uncle Theodore, Anne-Marie. Laxohyttan is the most beautiful place in the world. Come now, Anne-Marie!"

She raises her eyes. There are tears in them, and through the tears a glance full of despair and reproach falls on Maurits. She cannot understand; he insists upon going with an uncovered light into the powder magazine. Then she turns to Uncle Theodore; but not with the shy, childish manner she had before, but with a certain nobleness, with something of the martyr, of an imprisoned queen.

"You are much too good to us," she says only.

Thus is everything accomplished according to the demands of honor. There is not another word to be said in the matter. He has not robbed her of her faith in him whom she loves. She has not betrayed herself. She is faithful to him who has made her his betrothed, although she is only a poor girl from a little bakery in a back street.

And now the chaise can be brought up, the trunks be corded, the luncheon-basket filled.

Uncle Theodore leaves the table. He goes and places himself by a window. Ever since she has turned to him with that tearful glance he is out of his senses. He is quite mad, ready to throw himself upon her, press her to his breast and call to Maurits to come and tear her away if he can.

His hands are in his pockets. Through the clenched fists cramplike convulsions are passing.

Can he allow her to put on her hat, to say good-bye to the old lady?

There he stands again on the cliff of Naxos and wishes to steal the beloved for himself. Nor, not steal! Why not honorably and manfully step forward and say: "I am your rival, Maurits. Your betrothed must choose between us. You are not married; there is no sin in trying to win her from you. Look well after her. I mean to use every expedient."

Then he would be warned, and she would know what alternative lay before her.

His knuckles cracked when he clenched his fists again. How Maurits would laugh at his old uncle when he stepped forward and explained that! And what would be the good of it? Would he frighten her, so that he would not even be allowed to help them in the future?

But how will it go now when she approaches to say good-bye to him? He almost screams to her to take care, to keep three paces away from him.

He remains at the window and turns his back on them all, while they are busy with their wraps and their luncheon-basket. Will they never be ready to go? He has already lived it through a thousand times. He has taken her hand, kissed her, helped her into the chaise. He has done it so many times that he believes she is already gone.

He has also wished her happiness. Happiness – Can she be happy with Maurits? She has not looked happy this morning. Oh yes, certainly she has. She wept with joy.

While he is standing there Maurits suddenly says to Anne-Marie: "What a dunce I am! I am quite forgetting to speak to Uncle about father's shares."

"I think it would be best if you did not," Downie answers. "Perhaps it is not right."

"Nonsense, Anne-Marie. The shares do not pay anything just now. But who knows if they will not be better some day? And besides, what does it matter to Uncle? Such a little thing –"

She interrupts with unusual eagerness, almost anxiously. "I beg of you, Maurits, do not do it. Give in to me this once."

He looks at her, a little offended. "This once! – as if I were a tyrant over you. No, do you see. I cannot; just for that word I think that I ought not to yield."

"Do not cling to a word, Maurits. This means more than polite phrases. I think it is not well of you to wish to cheat Uncle now when he has been so good to us."

"Be quiet, Anne-Marie, be quiet! What do you understand of business?" His whole manner is now irritatingly calm and superior. He looks at her as a schoolmaster looks at a good pupil who is making a fool of himself at his examination.

"That you do not at all understand what is at stake!" she cries. And she strikes out despairingly with her hands.

"I really must talk to Uncle now," says Maurits, "if for nothing else, to show him that there is no question of any deceit. You behave so that Uncle can believe that I and my father are veritable cheats."

And he comes forward to his uncle and explains to him what these shares which his father wishes to sell him are. Uncle Theodore listens to him as well as he can. He understands instantly that his brother has made a bad speculation and wishes to protect himself from loss. But what of it, what of it? He is accustomed to render to the whole family connection such services. But he is not thinking of that, but of Downie. He wonders what is the meaning of that look of resentment she casts upon Maurits. It was not exactly love.

And so in the midst of his despair over the sacrifice he has to make, a faint glimmer of hope begins to rise up before him. He stands and stares at it like a man who is sleeping in a haunted room and sees a light mist rise from the floor and condense and grow and become a tangible reality.

"Come with me into my room, Maurits," he says; "you shall have the money immediately."

But while he speaks his eyes rest on Downie to see if the ghost can be prevailed upon to speak. But as yet he sees only dumb despair in her.

But he has hardly sat down by the desk in his room when the door opens and Anne-Marie comes in.

"Uncle Theodore," she says, very firmly and decidedly, "do not buy those papers!"

Ah, such courage, Downie! Who would have believed it of you who had seen you three days ago, when you sat at Maurits's side in the chaise and seemed to shrink and grow smaller for every word he said.

Now she needs all her courage, for Maurits is angry in earnest.

"Hold your tongue!" he hisses at her, and then roars to make himself heard by Uncle Theodore, who is sitting at his desk and counting notes. "What is the matter with you? The shares give no interest now; I have told Uncle that; but Uncle knows as well as I that they will pay. Do you think Uncle will let himself be cheated by one like me? Uncle surely understands those things better than any of us. Has it ever been my intention to give out these shares as good? Have I said anything but that for him who can wait it may be a good affair?"

Uncle Theodore says nothing; he only hands a package of notes to Maurits. He wonders if this will make the ghost speak.

"Uncle," says the little intractable proclaimer of the truth, for it is a known fact that no one can be more intractable than those soft, delicate creature when they are in the right, "these shares are not worth a shilling and will never be. We all know it at home there."

"Anne-Marie, you make me out a scoundrel!"

She surveys him all over as if her eyes were the moving blades of a pair of scissors, and she cuts off him bit by bit everything in which she had clothed him; and when at last she sees him in all the nakedness of egotism and selfishness, her terrible little tongue passes sentence upon him: –

"What else are you?"

"Anne-Marie!"

"Yes, what else are we both," continues the merciless tongue, which, since it has once started, finds it best to clear up this matter which has tortured her conscience ever since she has begun to realize that this rich man who owned this big estate had a heart too which could suffer and yearn. So while her tongue is so well started and all shyness seems to have fallen from her, she says: –

"When we placed ourselves in the chaise at home there, what did we think? What did we talk about on the way? About how we would deceive him there. 'You must be brave, Anne-Marie,' you said. 'And you must be crafty, Maurits,' I said. We thought only of ingratiating ourselves. We wished to have much and we wished to give nothing except hypocrisy. It was not our intention to say: 'Help us, because we are poor and care for one another,' but we were to flatter and fawn until Uncle was charmed by me or by you; that was our intention. But we meant to give nothing in return; neither love nor respect nor even gratitude. And why did you not come alone, why must I come too? You wished to show me to him; you wished me to – to –"

Uncle Theodore rises when he sees Maurits raise his hand against her. For now he has finished counting, and follows what is passing with his heart swelling with hope. His heart flies wide open to receive her as she now screams and runs into his arms, runs there without hesitation or consideration, quite as if there were no other place on earth to which to run.

"Uncle, he will strike me!"

And she presses close, close to him.

But Maurits is now calm again. "Forgive my impetuosity, Anne-Marie," he says. "It hurt me to hear you speak in such a childish way in Uncle's presence. But Uncle must also understand that you are only a child. Still I grant that not even the most just wrath gives a man the right to strike a woman. Come here now and kiss me. You need not seek protection from me with anybody."

She does not move, does not turn, only clings more closely.

"Downie, shall I let him take you?" whispers Uncle Theodore.

She answers only with a shudder, which quivers through him also.

Uncle Theodore feels so strong, so inspired. He, too, no longer sees his perfect nephew as before in the bright light of his perfection. He dares to jest with him.

"Maurits," he says, "you surprise me. Love makes you weak. Can you so promptly forgive her having called you a scoundrel? You must break with her instantly. Your honor, Maurits, think of your honor! Nothing in the world can permit a woman to insult a man. Place yourself in the chaise, my boy, and go away without this abandoned creature! It is only pure and simple justice after such an insult."

As he finishes this speech, he puts his big hands about her head and bends it back so that he can kiss her forehead.

"Give up this abandoned creature!" he repeats.

But now Maurits begins to understand also. He sees the light in Uncle Theodore's eyes and how one smile after the other dances over his lips.

"Come, Anne-Marie!"

She starts. Now he calls her as the man to whom she has promised herself. She feels she must obey. And she lets go of Uncle Theodore so suddenly that he cannot stop her, but she cannot go to Maurits; so she slides down to the floor and there she remains sitting and sobs.

"Go home alone in your chaise, Maurits," says Uncle Theodore sharply. "This young lady is guest in my house as yet, and I intend to protect her from your interference."

He no longer thinks of Maurits, but only to lift her up, dry her tears and whisper that he loves her.

Maurits, who sees them, the one weeping, the other comforting, cries: "Oh, this is a conspiracy! I am tricked! This is a comedy! You have stolen my betrothed from me and you mock me! You let me call one who never intends to come! I congratulate you on this affair, Anne-Marie!"

As he rushes out and slams the door, he calls back: "Fortune-hunter!"

Uncle Theodore makes a movement as if to go after him and chastise him, but Downie holds him back.

"Ah, Uncle Theodore, do let Maurits have the last word. Maurits is always right. Fortune-hunter, – that is just what I am, Uncle Theodore."

She creeps again close to him without hesitation, without question. And Uncle Theodore is quite confused; just now she was weeping and now she is laughing; just now she was going to marry one man and now she is caressing another. Then she lifts up her head and smiles: "Now I am your little dog. You cannot be rid of me."

"Downie," says Uncle Theodore with his gruffest voice: "You have known it the whole time!"

She began to whisper: "Had my brother –"

"And yet you wished, Downie – Maurits is lucky to be rid of you. Such a foolish, deceitful, hypocritical Downie, such an unreliable little wisp, such a, such a –"

Ah, Downie, ah, silken flower! You were certainly not a fortune-hunter only; you were also a fortune-giver, otherwise there would be nothing left of your happy peace in the house where you lived. To this day the garden is shaded by big beeches and the birch tree trunks stand there white and spotless from the root upwards. To this day the snake suns himself in peace on the slope, and in the pond in the park swims a carp which is so old that no boy has the heart to catch it. And when I come there, I feel that there is festival in the air, and it seems as if the birds and flowers still sang their beautiful songs of you.

Among the Climbing Roses

I could wish that the people with whom I have spent my summer would let their glance fall on these lines. Now when the cold, dark nights have come, I should like to carry their thoughts back to that bright, warm season.

Above all, I should like to remind them of the climbing-roses that enclosed the veranda, of the delicate, somewhat thin foliage of the clematis, which in the sunlight as well as in the moonlight was drawn in dark grey shadows on the light grey stone floor and threw a light lacelike veil over everything, and of its big, bright blossoms with their ragged edges.

Other summers remind me of fields of clover, or of birch-woods, or of apple trees and berry bushes, but that summer took its character from the climbing-roses. The bright, delicate buds, that could resist neither wind nor rain, the light, waving, pale-green shoots, the soft, bending stems, the exuberant richness of blossoms, the gaily humming hosts of insects, all follow me and rise up before me in their glory, when I think of that summer, that rosy, delicate, dainty summer.

Now, when the time for work has come, people often ask me how I passed my summer. Then everything glides from my memory, and it seems to me as if I had sat day in and day out on the veranda behind the climbing roses and breathed in fragrance and sunshine. What did I do? Oh, I watched others work.

There was a little upholsterer bee which worked from morning till night, from night till morning. From the soft, green leaves it sawed out a neat little oval with its sharp jaws, rolled it together as one rolls up a real carpet, and with the precious burden pressed to it, it fluttered away to the park and lighted on an old tree stump. There it burrowed down through dark passage-ways and mysterious galleries, until at last it reached the bottom of a perpendicular shaft. In its unknown depths, where neither ant nor centipede ever had ventured, it spread out the green leaf roll and covered the uneven floor with the most beautiful carpet. And when the floor was covered, the bee came back for new leaves to cover the walls of the shaft, and worked so quickly and eagerly, that there was soon not a leaf in the rose hedge that did not have an oval hole which bore testimony that it had been forced to assist in the adorning of the old tree-stump.

One fine day the little bee changed its occupation. It bored deep in among the ragged petals of the full-blown roses, sucked and drank all it could in those beautiful larders, and when it had got its fill, it flew quickly away to the old stump to fill the freshly-papered chambers with brightest honey.

The little upholsterer bee was not the only one who worked in the rose-bushes. There was also a spider, a quite unparalleled spider. It was bigger than any spider I have ever seen; it was bright orange with a clearly marked cross on its back, and it had eight long, red-and-white striped legs, all equally well marked. You ought to have seen it spin! Every thread was drawn out with the greatest precision from the first ones that were only for supports to the last fine connecting thread. And you should have seen it balance its way along the slender threads to seize a fly or to take its place in the middle of the web, motionless, patient, waiting for hours.

That big, orange spider won my heart; he was so patient and so wise. Every day he had his little encounter with the upholsterer bee, and he always came out of the affair with the same unfailing tact. The bee who took his way close by him caught time and time again in his net. Instantly it began to buzz and tear; it dragged at the fine web and behaved like a mad thing, which naturally resulted in its being more and more entangled and getting both legs and wings wound up in the sticky net.

As soon as the bee was exhausted and weakened, the spider came creeping out to it. It kept always at a respectful distance, but with the extreme end of one of the beautiful, red striped legs it gave the bee a little push, so that it swung round in the web. When the bee had again buzzed and raged itself tired, it received another gentle shove, and then another and yet another, until it spun round like a top and did not know what it was doing in its fury, and became so confused that it could not defend itself. But during the whirling the threads that held it fast twisted ever more tightly, till the tension became so great that they broke, and the bee fell to the ground. Yes, that was what the spider had wished, of course.

And that performance could they repeat, those two, day after day as long as the bee had work in the rose-bushes. Never could the little bee learn to look out for the spider-web, and never did the spider show anger or impatience. I liked them both; the little, eager, furry worker, as well as the big, crafty, old hunter.

Very few great events happened in the garden of the climbing roses. Between the espaliers one could see the little lake lying and twinkling in the sunlight. And it was a lake which was too little and too shut in to be able to heave in real waves, but at every little ripple on the grey surface thousands of small sparkles that glistened and played on the waves flew up; it seemed as if its depths had been full of fire that could not get out. And it was the same with the summer life there; it was usually so quiet, but if there came the slightest, little ripple – oh, how it could shine and glitter!

We needed nothing great to make us happy. A flower or a bird could make us merry for several hours, not to speak of the upholsterer bee. I shall never forget what pleasure I had once on his account.

The bee had been in the spider-web as usual, and the spider had as usual helped him out; but it had been fastened so securely that it had had to buzz a dreadfully long time and had been very tamed and subdued when it had flown away. I bent forward to see if the spider-web had suffered much damage. Fortunately it had not; but on the other hand a little yellow larva was caught in the web, a little threadlike monster, which consisted of only jaws and claws, and I was agitated, really agitated, at the sight of it.

I knew them, those May-bug larvae, that in thousands crawl up on the flowers and hide themselves under their petals. Did I not know them and yet admire them, those bold, cunning parasites, that sit hidden and wait, only wait, even if it is for weeks, until a bee comes, in whose yellow and black down they can hide. And did I not know their hateful skill just when the little cell-builder has filled a room with honey and on its surface laid the egg from which the rightful owner of the cell and the honey will come forth, just then to creep down on the egg and with careful balancing sit on it as on a boat; for if they should come down into the honey; they would drown. And while the bee covers the thimblelike cell with a green roof and carefully shuts in its young one, the yellow larva tears open n the egg with its sharp jaws and devours its contents, while the egg-shell has still to serve as craft on the dangerous honey-sea.

But gradually the little yellow larva grows flat and big and can swim by itself on the honey acid drink of it, and in the course of time a fat, black beetle comes out of the bee-cell. It is certain that this is not what the little bee wished to effect by its work, and however cunningly and cleverly the beetle may have behaved, it is nevertheless nothing but a lazy parasite, who deserves no sympathy.

And my bee, my own little, industrious bee, bad flown about with such a yellow hanger-on in its down. But while the spider had spun round with it, the larva had loosened and fallen down on the spider-web, and now the big, orange spider came and gave it a bite and transformed it in a second into a skeleton without life or substance.

When the little bee came again, its humming was like a hymn to life.

"Oh, thou beauteous life," it said. "I thank thee that happy work among roses and sunshine has fallen to my lot. I thank thee that I can enjoy thee without anxiety or fear.

"Well I know that spiders lie in wait and beetles steal, but happy work is mine, and brave freedom from care. Oh, thou beauteous life, thou glorious existence!"

www.ingramcontent.com/pod-product-compliance
Lightning Source LLC
Chambersburg PA
CBHW030418310726
48979CB00007B/1103

* 9 7 8 1 5 9 8 1 8 1 4 5 6 *